# KRISTA'S DILEMMA

## GEMMA JACKSON

POOLBEG

Published 2021
by Poolbeg Press Ltd.
123 Grange Hill, Baldoyle,
Dublin 13, Ireland
Email: poolbeg@poolbeg.com

A catalogue record for this book is available from the British Library.

ISBN 978178199-459-7

www.poolbeg.com

## Also by Gemma Jackson

*Through Streets Broad and Narrow*
*Ha'penny Chance*
*The Ha'penny Place*
*Ha'penny Schemes*
*Impossible Dream*
*Dare to Dream*
*Her Revolution*

Published by Poolbeg

# Foreword

Dear Reader,

I hope you enjoy the latest in Krista's journey. I have so much fun researching the background of these stories that sometimes I get lost and go off at a tangent and have to drag myself back. What amazing men and women our ancestors were!

My character Krista is an illegitimate child. Many of my readers may find the reaction of other characters to this fact unbelievable. May I hold up my hand and say I know what I am writing about! I am not so much fascinated as touched by the fate of illegitimate children in the past – in fact, until very recently. Both my parents were what was coyly referred to as 'war babies'. They were raised within their family units so each knew the facts of their birth. I was witness to the pain inflicted on them by rules, regulations and unintended social cruelty. As my parents' child I too was snubbed and ignored. It didn't bother me all that much. I did get angry on my parents' behalf from time to time. In my youth I caused ructions at social events in their defence. What child wouldn't defend her parents? I couldn't understand the attitude of many to my parents – the child is innocent.

In this story I make a passing reference to a woman whose life story has always fascinated me. Margaretha Geertruida Zelle McLeod AKA Mata Hari. This woman is portrayed in books and films – her story has been glamorised until the truth is lost. As a young girl Margaretha sought adventure. When I read about her, I find myself almost banging my head off the nearest hard object and screaming *Noooooo!* It doesn't change anything but it makes me feel better.

So, come along with me as I weave my way around the happenings in the lead-up to the Second World War.

I hope you enjoy reading the stories as much as I am enjoying writing them.

Gemma

# Chapter 1

Felixstowe Dock
November 1938

Krista stood on the dock waiting for the campervan that had been her home for the last two weeks to be off-loaded from the ferry. Her travelling companions through Germany and Belgium, Perry and Gisele, were waiting in the first-class passengers, lounge for the arrival of the family whom they had telegraphed from Antwerp.

She was glad of the time alone. She needed to think. What was she going to do now? She had stood on this dock just six months ago, unsure of her future. She was still unsure in spite of meeting people who wished to help her. They had been kind but she had been moved around like a chess piece – always at the direction of others. She needed to take her fate in her own hands. But how?

She had money in a Post Office account. She had been paid – what to her was a great deal of money – to travel to Germany and rescue Gisele Waters, the twin sister of Captain Waters of the armed forces. She had completed that mission. Was she now free to pursue her own interests? But what were those interests? Surely she should know.

She absentmindedly moved the gold wedding band from her left hand to her right. She had been travelling as a married woman, with Peregrine Fotheringham-Carter posing as her husband. She was eighteen years old – that was, in her opinion, far too young to be married.

"*Krista!*"

The sound of her name jerked her out of her introspection. She turned to search for the person calling to her.

"Miss Andrews!"

What was her former English language teacher and one of the people who accompanied her from France six months ago doing on this dock? The upright slim older woman wearing a navy-blue skirt-suit marched practically in military fashion towards her.

"Violet, my dear." She examined the younger woman, vastly relieved to see her here in one piece. "I have appointed myself your guardian, you know, and as such I insist you call me Violet."

"Violet," Krista said, "what are you doing here?"

"I travelled down from London with Admiral Sir Henry Fotheringham-Carter, Perry's father." Violet pinched the sleeve of the oiled hip-length jacket Krista was wearing. "What on earth are you wearing, my dear?

I understood you were given a wardrobe of superior ladies' garments for this charade." She scrunched up her nose at the waterproof slacks, boots and jacket that were not her idea of what a well-brought-up young lady should be wearing.

"I was," Krista laughed. "I got little chance to wear them. We were winter camping after all. These," she gestured towards her outfit, "were of far more use for the situation I found myself in." Thankfully she was to be allowed to keep the wardrobe of expensive luggage and clothing. They would serve her well as she planned her future.

"The admiral has arranged with the dockmaster for a room to be set aside for his use." Violet had insisted on accompanying the admiral. "He wishes to debrief Perry and yourself. I received the impression that he was not pleased his son was sent off on a dangerous mission without his knowledge or consent."

"Perry is twenty years old." Krista watched the campervan being hoisted into the air and carried off the deck of the ferry. "Surely he does not need parental consent?"

"He is not yet twenty-one, my dear." Violet stared at the strange vehicle above their heads. "I will admit I was concerned to hear that you were travelling as a married couple. Did you give no thought to your reputation?"

"What reputation?" Krista turned her attention to the woman who had helped her escape her nightmare situation in France. The woman who had told her the truth about her natural parents. She owed a great deal to Violet Andrews. "I am nothing and no-one. Why should I be concerned with what people I don't know and don't care about think of me?"

"It is difficult, Krista, to be a woman alone." Violet's pale-blue eyes narrowed. "One has to be vigilant in protecting one's good name. There is a certain type of man –"

"*Krista!*" A shout from behind halted Violet's words.

The two women turned to see Perry walking towards them. His tall, broad-shouldered figure was wrapped in clothing similar to Krista's. His thick brown hair blew back from his chiselled features. His light-brown, almost amber eyes were narrowed against the glare of the light off the sea. He had been using crutches after a bad horse-riding accident when Krista first met him. He walked confidently now with almost no hitch in his stride.

"Captain Waters has arrived," Perry said as he reached them. "Miss Andrews, I had not expected to see you here." He flashed his twin dimples, eyebrow raised as he waited for Miss Andrews to explain her presence on the dock.

"I was involved in talks with the Admiralty when your father received your telegram, Perry." Violet had met this young man many times at the home of Krista's employers, the Caulfields. "I asked to accompany him in case Krista had need of me."

"My father has arranged for a private room." Perry gestured with one arm, inviting the ladies to accompany him back towards the dockside building. "He wishes to speak with the three people who have just arrived from Germany. I imagine Captain Waters is not best pleased to have my father interfere." Perry laughed. "But he outranks him."

"Indeed." Violet had no intention of being put on the side-lines. She and her fellow ex-Wrens had been in talks with the Admiralty for months. It had been a time of deep frustration as they endeavoured to get hard-headed men to listen to them. The Admiralty had agreed to allow women to volunteer for duties such as catering, office duties and motor transport. There had been no mention so far of reinstating the Women's Royal Naval Service. Violet and women like her who had served in the Great War were beating their heads against a brick wall. The men in power could not be made to see that the Wrens would be a vital force in whatever was to come.

Admiral Sir Henry Fotheringham-Carter was an impressive figure, very much an older copy of his youngest son. He stood at the front of the room – some sort of classroom judging from the set-up. The others stood in a group in front of him. He glared from under beetling brows at Violet and Krista, obviously wondering what business the two women had in this company.

"Now that we are all here, I would like to hear all that has been discovered. I would also like to know," here he glared at Captain Waters and his twin sister Gisele, "why this mission was not discussed in detail with the intelligence sector of the armed forces."

"I discussed the particulars of the situation with my superiors in Army Intelligence, sir." Captain Waters stood at parade rest although he was wearing civilian clothing.

"We cannot go forward with this type of attitude," said the admiral. "We need all of the intelligence we can gather. It is shameful that the navy had no knowledge of your endeavour." Which wasn't strictly true in his case. He had known his youngest son was involved in covert operations.

"I agree, sir, but until such time as we have a central bureau for gathering intelligence, each force will continue to gather what information they may." Captain Waters had long thought it was ridiculous that the British Forces did not have a designated force-wide Intelligence Service. One was needed now more than ever.

"Surely that conversation is for another time and place." Violet had been listening to men just like these beating their chests and rattling their sabres for months. They achieved nothing. "We are here to discuss the findings of the three people who have just arrived back in the country. Are we not?" It was liberating not to have to adhere to the strict rules and regulations of people in uniform. The navy refused to acknowledge the contribution of women like her, so for the moment she would refuse to acknowledge the hierarchy of the navy. She raised her chin and glared at the admiral.

"Quite so," the admiral growled. "Waters, what was the purpose of sending my son and this ..." he waved towards Krista, "this person into Germany."

"My sister Gisele ..." Waters pinched the bridge of his nose. How much should he tell? What was the procedure here? He represented a different branch of the armed forces from the Admiral. Should he discuss matters openly with someone who was not in his direct line of command?

"Graham," Gisele touched the sleeve of her brother's

jacket, "the admiral needs to know."

"Admiral, my sister is a scientist." He stopped when the older man growled in apparent disbelief.

"Father!" Perry knew his father was not one to believe women should stay in the kitchen. How could he be with a wife like Perry's mother? A woman who had served her country in the Great War in ways that could never be revealed.

"I apologise, captain." Sir Henry waved his hand, inviting the captain to continue.

"My sister is a skilled scientist. She has made remarkable studies of the uses of gases and bacteria in both healing and weaponry." Graham looked at his twin.

"I mean no disrespect to anyone here but –" the admiral stared at the nondescript little woman shrouded in widow's weeds, standing so quietly by the side of the man who was apparently her twin, "I take a keen interest in the sciences and, as such, I have never heard of Gisele Waters." The admiral harrumphed.

"You will perhaps have heard of my husband." Gisele pulled the unattractive chamber-pot-shaped black hat off. It wasn't much of an improvement as her blonde hair was stuck to her head. She had been travelling and sleeping rough in the clothes she wore for what felt like months. "Herr Professor Maxim von Snyder is well known in some circles."

"Sweet Lord!" The admiral leaned forward. "Professor Maxim von Snyder? You are claiming to be that great man's wife? The man is a world-renowned genius." He turned with clenched fists towards Captain Waters and through gritted teeth growled, "Why on earth did you not get that man out of Hitler's clutches? He is exactly the type of man we need on our side in the coming conflict. I simply cannot believe that you had close contact with von Snyder and instead rescued his – wife!" He almost spat the final word, glaring at the group gathered before him as if doubting their sanity.

The sound of Perry's laughter cut through the staring contest the captain and admiral were engaged in, both men refusing to back down.

"Son!" the admiral snapped. "This is no time for levity."

Perry pushed a hand through his hair. He was tired. The journey to rescue Gisele had been dangerously stressful. He wanted a stiff drink, a bath and a week's worth of sleep. "Father, you are barking up the wrong tree. Von Snyder is not the genius here."

"*Explain.*" The admiral knew he was missing something and he was not a man who liked to be out of the loop.

"Herr Professor Maxim von Snyder may well be a man of letters but he is no genius." Perry exchanged an understanding glance with Captain Waters. The truth needed to be made known. "What the good professor appears to be excellent at is putting his name to his students' research. The published articles I imagine you have read with interest, Father, were all works completed by his wife. The man merely put his name to his wife's body of work." He turned to the woman he had been instrumental in removing from danger and with a slight bow of the head said, "I am sorry, Gisele, but your husband sounds like a charlatan to me."

"Can something so preposterous possibly be true?" the admiral demanded.

Captain Graham Waters said nothing. He had long been holding back his opinion of his twin's husband. In his opinion the much older man took advantage of a shy young student. His sister had never spoken against her husband. Graham did not want his twin's marriage to cause a rift between them.

"That is not so surprising." Violet Andrews had been listening closely. "It has long been an established custom for men to claim credit for a wife's genius. Female artists, scientists, writers, all have had their work brought to the public under a man's name. It is sometimes the only way for them to continue with their work."

Krista wondered how long she would have to stand here and listen. She was exhausted.

"There is much we need to discuss – I will have an explanation." The admiral beat the tabletop with his open hand, glaring at the captain and his sister.

"You are not my commanding officer, sir," Graham Waters said softly.

"Father –" Perry broke into the uncomfortable silence. He wanted to get on the road home. His father was capable of keeping them all dancing to his tune for hours. "Those of us who travelled are tired, dirty and hungry. There is much you need to know but perhaps the conversation could take place after we have all rested?" He knew by his father's clenched jaw that he was going to dig his heels in, so added hastily, "I met a man in Germany who claimed to know you. Herr Count Johann Graf Benz."

"Fine sailor, lovely family, I know him well." The admiral allowed himself to be distracted.

"Graf Benz went out of his way to show us," Perry gestured to Krista with one hand, "a gathering of a great number of deadly submarines. The U-boats Krista and I observed are berthed in waters that will allow them to attack many nations' waterways. I believe the man wanted me to share the information with you."

"Dear Lord," the admiral looked around the gathering, "I came here today to fetch my youngest son." He sighed, shaking his head. "It would appear I have stepped into a hornet's nest instead."

"We observed a great deal that is of much concern to our government." Perry wanted his father to step aside and allow Captain Waters to debrief them. They had travelled to Germany on his orders after all.

"Captain, I will set up an appointment with General Lord Mortimore, commander of the armed forces. I want you and your sister at that meeting," the admiral said. "I will talk with my son about his findings. He too will be at the meeting and he will let you know the time and place."

"Perry must return to his studies," Captain Waters objected. "Time is of the essence. We are going to need men like your son trained up and fluent in the languages of the Continent."

"Hitler is dangerous – of that there can be no doubt – but of everything we have seen of him the man is not a fool," the admiral said. "We are deep into winter. He will not begin his march to victory in winter conditions. He is waiting for spring. We will have to be ready for him when he does decide to attack his neighbours." He had no doubt that the following year, 1939, would see Hitler strike. Hitler could not afford to keep all of the soldiers he was rumoured to have commissioned within his own border lines. An army could not remain at peak condition while waiting around for action. There was a danger some of your army might turn its deadly attention to your own people. From accounts reported in the newspapers there was already general unrest in Germany.

"Our Prime Minister Neville Chamberlin is convinced that he has brokered peace," Graham Waters said softly.

"The man is a fool to believe Hitler and all here know it." Admiral Sir Henry Fotheringham-Carter glared at the company, daring anyone to disagree with him.

# Chapter 2

"Krista, Perry, one of my men removed your belongings from the campervan." Graham Waters wanted to get his sister home where they would discuss the happenings in Germany in greater comfort. He needed to know everything she knew. His sister had a way of looking at the world that was different from the average female. "Your belongings have been left in the dockmaster's office. The campervan is being returned to base as we speak."

Krista walked over to the window looking down on the dockyard. The campervan was gone! She was shocked to realise she would miss their mobile home. What was she to do now? She stood staring down at the busy scene below her, ignoring the conversations being held in the room behind her.

Violet Andrews joined Krista at the window. She had nothing to add to the conversations. She would keep out of the way and watch and listen. One heard a great deal when people forgot you were present.

"You have completed your first mission, Perry." Graham stood close to Perry while the admiral spoke with his twin. "I look forward to reading your report." He nodded in the direction of Krista. "How did she do?"

"She was amazing." Perry smiled. "I told her she had a career as a writer of fiction ahead of her." He laughed with genuine amusement. "You should have heard the stories she told of her ancestor Brunhilda Alvensleben ..."

"Who?"

"She invented a life for her fictitious ancestor. She had me almost convinced I knew the woman." Perry looked at the stiff back of his travelling companion. "She handled the soldiers and guards with a smile and an innocence that she had to fight hard to project. She never faltered. I was merely her sidekick, as the film cowboys say."

"So, war is coming ..." Graham Waters had never doubted it.

The two men spoke briefly of all Perry had seen and heard. Perry felt his insides clench as he tried to imagine how he would report the horrors he had witnessed. How could he possibly share his reaction to the night he was forced to stand by and watch as men women and children were pulled from their homes by laughing soldiers. He would be spared actually having to write about the horrific happenings of the 10th of November. He had read the newspaper reports on board ship. They were calling it "Crystal Night" because of the sounds of breaking glass, it seemed.

Krista walked over to join them. She stood silently listening as Perry spoke – she had little to add. Perry had great difficulty expressing his impression of all that he had seen and experienced that night of nightmare.

"You both did far better than I ever imagined you would," Graham said when Perry wound down his recounting. "I can never thank you both enough for getting my twin home safely."

"What now, captain?" Krista asked when Perry remained silent.

"I believe this belongs to you." Graham took a British passport from his inside breast pocket and passed it to Krista. "You are now officially a British citizen. You are free to move around the country."

Krista took the passport, unable to form words. She was legal! No one could force her to leave the country she hoped to make her home. She had travelled through Europe on papers showing her as Perry's wife. She held no legal documents of her own, having fled France with only the clothes on her back. She would not apply for legal documents from France for fear of exposing her whereabouts to the Dumas family – something she would prefer not to do. Now she held a British passport in her own name. She wanted to dance. She had options open to her now that she held proof of her citizenship. Her mind whirled – what would she do?

"Captain," the admiral had joined them, "I need to leave. There is much to be done. I will take my son with me. I want to speak with him further. You have my details." The admiral turned away, expecting everyone to jump to it at his words.

Krista felt invisible. This was a huge moment for her. She longed to share the joy of having a legal passport in her hand but no one seemed to care.

"Your son, sir, needs to report back to his base." Graham Waters' words stopped the admiral in his tracks.

Sir Henry turned and the two men locked eyes for a moment.

"I will return him to base after I have spoken to him," he said.

"He has a written report to prepare and submit," Graham objected.

"His mother will type up his report before it is presented to you," Sir Henry said over his shoulder as he walked towards the exit to the room. "Perry, with me!"

"Sir –" Perry looked between the two men, not sure what the protocol was here. His father outranked the captain but the mission he had just completed was at the captain's command.

"Go." Graham Waters wanted to get Gisele away from here.

"Krista, will you see to my belongings?" Perry asked.

"*No need!*" Sir Henry shouted impatiently. "I had my man put your haversack in the car. Come along, Perry, time is fleeing!"

"I'll see you soon, Krista." Perry walked backwards after his father. He stared at her, not wanting to say farewell under these circumstances. He knew better than to disobey his father, though, when he was in full admiral mode. "I'll need help with my languages homework." He turned and swiftly left.

"Krista, thank you." Gisele Waters was at her twin's side. She looked so frail, standing beside the taller man.

"Yes, Krista, thank you," Graham Waters said. "The harbour master will arrange a car to the train station for you and Miss Andrews."

With that, he put his arm around Gisele and almost towed her from the room.

Violet Andrews walked over to join Krista.

"Peggy would say that was very much 'Here's your hat, what's your hurry?'," Krista said, staring around the room, empty now except for herself and Violet.

"Peggy Matthews has a good head on her shoulders. I have always found maidservants speak a great deal of sense. The Caulfields are fortunate to have her in their employ." She pressed her hand to the passport, smiling with pleasure. "I am so glad that your papers have come through." She and her friend Abigail had fought long and hard to secure Krista's right to stay in the country of her mother's birth.

"I feel like a balloon with all of the air leaking out of it." Krista stared at the passport in her hand. It offered her a freedom she had not had before. "I don't know where to go or what to do."

"Cordelia Caulfield and her boys have missed you greatly. It would perhaps make sense to spend the winter with them?" Violet could not afford to house and feed Krista. She was barely keeping herself afloat financially.

"Did you hear Perry ask me to help with his homework?" Krista wanted to kick something. "I was right there," she pointed vaguely over her shoulder. "I speak French, German and English – fluently – yet Captain Waters spoke of the great need for people to speak Continental languages – but he never mentioned me!" She beat her chest with the side of her clenched fist.

"He spoke of men, my dear." Violet almost laughed. She'd had the same frustrations herself growing up. It seemed nothing had changed. "You do not qualify."

"But it is so unfair!" Krista wailed.

"Who ever said life was fair?" Violet took Krista's elbow. "Come away, child. We need to pick up your luggage and get to the train station."

"To go where?"

"We will discuss the matter on the train." Violet began to walk towards the exit.

"I feel surplus to requirements." Krista, having been forced by Miss Andrews to change her clothes in the Harbour Master's office – the woman refused to travel with her dressed in her oiled outfit – was wearing her navy-blue dress and coat.

The two women were sitting in the first-class carriage of the train. They had the carriage to themselves. They sat facing each other on the soft brown bench-style seats as the English countryside flashed past outside the window.

"It is the way of the world, I'm afraid, my dear." Violet almost smiled at the disgruntled look on the younger woman's face. "You know I served in the Wrens with your mother and Abigail, Lady Winchester." She put her arm on the sill under the window. She leaned against the glass and looked out briefly before returning her eyes to her travelling companion. She didn't wait for a response to her question but, laughing gently at the memory, she continued. "I was so young, so sure of my own importance. I became involved in setting up the Wrens when the call went out for women to serve in the Great War. I spent years commanding women who were willing to lay down their lives for their country – many did in fact die during that conflict – but their courage and sacrifice was forgotten as soon as the war ended." Violet sighed deeply. The child didn't want a history lesson. "We were vital to the war effort. We won the right to wear uniforms and insignia that matched our male counterparts. We learned to march in formation. We were sailors." She slapped her hand against the windowsill. "Then we were nothing! Surplus to requirements, as you have said. We fought it. We begged to be allowed to continue."

"Is that why you decided to live in France?" Krista prompted when Violet fell silent and stared out the window.

"Yes." Violet laughed bitterly. "I was pouting. My country had rejected me so I rejected my country." She shook her head at her own vanity. As if anyone cared what she did or where she went. "I am frustrated. Once more our country is marching towards war. The signs are all there for everyone to see. Yet the powers that be are refusing to see that the Wrens and women's services will once more be called to action." She beat her hand on the windowsill hard enough to bruise it. "We need to start training up this generation to function as a well-trained force but no-one wants to listen to us. We will need women like you to join us."

"You want me to become a Wren?" This was the first Krista had heard of it. "I am no sailor. I had never seen the sea until I ran away from home."

"It will be your language skills that will be of most importance. It is a rare thing for someone to be fluent in three languages – English, French and German. People like you will be vital to the forces."

"It is not such a rare thing in Europe." Krista also knew a smattering of Italian and Spanish but had made no mention of it as she wasn't fluent in those languages.

"We will need you, Krista," Violet insisted. "When the powers that be realise that women in the forces will once more be needed, I want you available to the Wrens. Whenever that comes to pass."

"Captain Waters and the admiral may be able to bring matters to the attention of the men in power." Krista hated to see Violet so upset.

"Yes." Again the windowsill was slapped. "*Because they are men!*"

The two women sat watching the countryside, each lost in her own thoughts. The train journey from Felixstowe in Suffolk to London was not a long one.

"Krista, you need to make plans," Violet said when the scenery outside the window began to change as they approached London. "I have managed to survive as a woman alone but it has been difficult. I cannot offer you financial assistance but I am available to offer advice if you would care to take it?"

"I cannot imagine returning to looking after Lia's boys," Krista said. "I am grateful for the time I have spent with the Caulfield family. I owe them a great deal. I have learned so much in the months I spent in the Caulfield house. Peggy and Mrs Acers the cook took me in hand. I knew nothing about taking care of my possessions. I was spoiled though I didn't know it. I had the *auberge* workers to take care of so much of the day-to-day chores. Peggy taught me to rinse out my smalls." Krista laughed. "You should have seen her face when I expected her to take care of my laundry!"

Violet laughed with her. "I have never given thought to that but, yes, you grew up in what was essentially a hotel. The maids took care of cleaning. The hotel laundry would take care of your clothes. The kitchen staff would supply your food needs. Why, you were practically a babe-in-arms as far as knowing how to take care of yourself was concerned." She thought of all the girls from privileged backgrounds – who if they joined the Wrens would have to learn some of what Krista had learned.

"I learned. I had to." Krista was grateful to the women who had taken the time to show her how to take care of her own daily needs. "I have grown fond of Lia, her family and staff, but I need something that is mine. Somewhere that is mine. Can you understand?"

"Krista," Violet sighed, "you are eighteen years old. You have all of your life in front of you. You cannot sit here and make decisions that affect the rest of your life.

Surely you have seen that, with what you experienced during the time you spent in France and your recent visit to Germany? No one knows what the next day will bring." She leaned forward and put her hand on Krista's knee. "You have time. You have money in the Post Office. The only way to have money, my dear, is not to spend it! The Caulfield family offer you a place to stay and food to eat. Believe me when I tell you those two items eat up any money you may have. Take the winter to think over what you want to do."

"What do I say about my absence from the house? I don't want to lie to people who have treated me with nothing but kindness. Everyone was told I was visiting distant relatives. What do I say about that?" Krista knew Lia was aware of her recent task but the household had been told Krista was visiting English relatives. "I was not told what I can and cannot say about my recent journey." She beat the windowsill too, hoping it might help ease her frustration. It didn't. "Perry is required to submit a written report. But I was thanked, patted on the head and sent on my way."

"Get used to it, my dear," Violet said as the train slowed to pull into the station. She stood and swayed with the motion. "We will need a porter for your luggage. Are you willing to return to the Caulfield house?"

"I suppose so." Krista sounded like a sulky child even to her own ears.

# Chapter 3

Caulfield House
Knightsbridge
London

"Are you sure you will be alright on your own?" Lia Caulfield, an elegant woman wearing brown tweed slacks with a peach knit twinset, stood in the open doorway of her twin sons' bedroom. Her pale-blue eyes stared at the young woman packing bags for her sons. "I feel frightfully guilty leaving you alone at Christmas."

"I will be fine." Krista laughed. "Christmas does not mean as much to me as it appears to mean to English people. I will enjoy the time on my own, I promise you." In France the sixth of December was important to children. It was the day Papa Noel came to visit. She had been surprised when informed the English did not celebrate the day. For the French, the most important celebration was the New Year.

"The boys are looking forward to spending time with their grandmother." Lia walked into the room and took a seat on one of the twin beds. "She spoils them so."

"Lia," Krista paused in her packing to stare at the woman who employed her and was becoming something of a friend and advisor, "you should give serious thought to the twins and yourself moving to the country when you are away." Captain Caulfield's family had a large estate on the Norfolk coast. A large area of wild beauty, from what she could gather.

"Live with my mother-in-law!" Lia gasped. "I would go insane inside of a week."

"Is there not a fisherman's or farm cottage you could make use of?" Krista examined the two suitcases she had open on one of the twin beds. It was vital to pack the same items in each case. There would be a mini-war if David and Edward discovered that they did not have identical items on hand.

"The boys and me in a cottage!" Lia laughed. "It does not bear thinking about."

Krista closed the two cases and put them on the floor. She sat on the bed and stared across the stretch of blue carpet to Lia on the other bed. "Lia, you will be away for two weeks. I am not suggesting you move now but, really, you must give serious thought to getting the boys and yourself out of London."

"What you have told me and what I read in the newspapers scares me stiff, Krista." Lia put her elbows on her slacks-covered knees and leaned forward. "My husband is captain of a naval ship. I am terrified of what a war could mean for him. Putting that to one side, I don't believe Norfolk would be a safe place for the twins. It is a major port after all and whispers of factories and airfields being installed have come to the ears of the workers on the estate. Nowhere will be truly safe but surely the twins and I will be safe here in London?"

"I am not saying war will break out next week," Krista insisted. "Those in the know appear to think Hitler will wait for winter to pass before he makes a move. But, Lia," she leaned forward, spearing Lia with her startlingly blue eyes, "he will move and Britain will have to react. It has promised to support its neighbours in time of trouble."

"But Prime Minister Chamberlin –"

"Is dreaming," Krista bit out before Lia could once again trot out Chamberlain's belief in the word of Adolf Hitler.

"I was a young child when the Great War broke out." Lia closed her eyes briefly. "I was not supposed to understand the world around me. But I did understand. How would it be possible not to understand the death of young men who had visited my family home. The despair and sadness of the adults." She pushed trembling hands through her dark-brown hair. "I cannot believe we are once more facing into such horror."

"Lia, so many people are closing their eyes to what is happening." Krista had seen and heard a great deal as she worked in the café/bar/tabac of the Auberge du Ville in Metz on the French-German border. She did not have the luxury of ignoring what was taking place in the world around her. "You cannot be one of them. You have two charming young boys to protect. David and Edward must come first."

"I am frightened."

"We all are."

"Krista, I am not the sort of woman to sit safely in a cottage while the world around me runs mad. If my country does go to war I want to do my bit." Lia had lain awake nights wondering what contribution she could make to the war effort.

"The work you and your friends have done for the children of Germany and Austria has been remarkable. But, Lia, have you thought of the effect war will have on the children of Britain. You are in a fortunate position. You can afford to escape to the country and wait out the war if that is your wish. Think of people like Peggy's family. They will have to stay in London if no one offers them a choice. So many people offered to take the children you rescued and continue to rescue from the Continent. What about the British children? What is to become of them?" Krista stared at Lia, waiting for the other woman to realise that there was still a great deal of work to do to ensure the safety of the young.

"You have given me a great deal to think about." Lia stood. "In the Great War Norfolk was bombed from the air. Who is to say this will not happen again? I will spend time thinking about what the future might bring. I believe I will speak with people who witnessed the explosion of the zeppelins in the Great War, what people took to calling flying ships. Such a dangerous thing, a great big balloon filled with dangerous gasses floating through the sky. It was the efforts of the Royal Flying Corps that saved us then." She sighed. "It is so hard to prepare for the unknown. Still, what will be will be. The car will be here early in the morning. I want to check my bags one more time. But I will give careful thought to all you have said."

"Lia," Krista thought in for a penny in for a pound, "you might consider learning to drive around the estate while you are there. Captain Caulfield will not be home for the full two weeks. It will give you something to concentrate on." The other woman was becoming increasingly nervous and frustrated. The world around them felt as if everyone was holding their breath waiting to see what would happen.

"You are determined to force me out of the blues." Lia laughed. "I would enjoy learning to drive. It is a skill that may serve me well."

Krista stood on the front path with Peggy and Mrs Acers, waving goodbye to the family. The luxury car, followed by the van holding the family's luggage, was soon around the corner and out of sight. With a sigh the three women went back inside, closing the main house door at their backs.

"I'll put the kettle on," Mrs Acers said. "Come into the kitchen the pair of you and join me. We've been running around like blue-arsed flies all morning. You would think the family was sailing around the world from the fuss they made." She was still speaking as the kitchen door closed at her back.

"It's well for them going to the sea for Christmas,"

Peggy said. "I wouldn't mind joining them."

"Do you not wish to spend Christmas with your family?" Krista pushed the kitchen door open as she spoke.

"Krista, you're a caution!" Mrs Acers laughed at Krista's words.

"I don't understand." Krista began to set the kitchen table. "What does that mean?"

"It means you're funny – amusing," said Peggy.

"Peggy, put some toast on," said Mrs Acers. "There was so much commotion this morning the bit I ate is stuck in me throat." She watched the kettle, willing it to boil. She needed a pot of tea.

"Why is what I said amusing?" Krista asked.

"You have this big house all around you, Krista." Peggy sliced a loaf of bread. "Can you imagine being in a little house? We have three bedrooms, a front parlour me mam won't let anyone sit in, a privy down the back and twelve people fighting for space. It sometimes feels as if all the air has gone before you have a chance to take a deep breath." Not to mention the fighting that went on over every little thing and her da sitting like the Lord Mayor expecting to be waited on hand and foot. She put the bread in the toaster, marvelling anew at the little machine. Her mam made toast holding the bread in front of the open door of her range.

"You have a false sense of people living in this house, Krista." Wilma Acers carried the teapot to the table, glad to get off her feet as her corns were giving her gyp. "To me and Peggy working in this house is a little blessing. We have full and plenty, never questioned about what we eat and drink. Not all big houses are that generous with their staff. The Caulfields are lovely people. She doesn't stand on ceremony, despite the fact she comes from money and her family is titled. You don't know you're born landing in with the Caulfields, I can tell you, girl."

"The house is going to get a deep cleaning while the family is away, Krista." Peggy carried the toast to the table. "With you being here to oversee and pay the workers, the missus told me I could go home but I don't want to." She thumped down onto the wooden chair.

"Lia left me written instructions and a stack of small brown wage envelopes to hand out to the workers when they complete their work. I will be glad of your company, Peggy. You can tell me who is who." Krista knew the two women who scrubbed the house out weekly and the washerwoman of course but there were a great many more names on the list Lia had left with her. She had been left with cash that she would have to keep careful account of too.

"I'll look forward to seeing the place shining like a new penny when I come back," Wilma Acers said. "I have paid holidays, which is a rare thing I can tell you." She nodded her head firmly. "I have family coming for the holidays. I have to get the house ready and the food in. There will be no-one offering to help me get the food on the table. I'll be busier than ever."

The three women settled down to enjoy their morning snack and catch up on any gossip going about the people living around them. The servants saw a lot more than their employers ever knew. Krista listened, not really knowing the people they were talking about. She felt guilty. She had been mentally moaning about her lot in life since she returned from Germany.

"Will you be seeing Perry over the holidays?" Peggy's voice jerked Krista back to earth.

"I doubt it. Perry has a great many family obligations over the holidays."

"You know, you could have that man just like *that!*" Peggy clicked her fingers together, the sound loud in the kitchen.

"I am too young to be seriously courting." Krista knew Peggy thought the world of Perry. He treated her with humour and respect which she seemed to enjoy.

"You're right." Wilma Acers nodded. "You give yourself time to enjoy life before you settle down, my girl. There's no need to be rushing off to get wed. You've time and plenty for that sort of thing."

"I thought you were married at seventeen, Wilma Acers!" Peggy snapped.

"And so I was," Wilma said. "So, it's the voice of experience here, my girl. You take the time to kick up your heels before you tie yourself down to a man and children."

"I don't know if I ever want to wed." Peggy was thinking of her mother. An old woman at forty with all them children and a demanding husband. Her mother never complained but Peggy had seen a different way of life and wasn't willing to settle down with any of the demanding young men that came calling to her parents' home. She wanted someone like Perry. She'd never have a man from such exalted social circles but surely there was a man somewhere who wouldn't expect her to be his slave?

"You'll change your mind when the right man comes along," Wilma said with a sharp nod of her head. "But wait for the right one. Don't rush into anything just for the sake of getting married."

"Mrs Acers is right, Peggy. We have time on our side." Krista put her hand over hers. "I am eighteen and you are only twenty-two. We have plenty of time to make life-long decisions."

"In my neck of the woods twenty-two is over the hill and on the shelf!" Peggy laughed. She did like Krista but the girl hadn't a clue what the real world was like.

"It appears to me that, with all we are hearing from that lot on the wireless and in the newspapers, you two will be forced to make some decisions – and soon." Wilma needed to get on. She had her own home to see to. She pushed her chair back from the table before standing. She looked down at the two young women staring up at her. It didn't bear thinking about that these two would see a world at war. The last lot was supposed to be "the war to end all wars". It wasn't even twenty years since the lads came home – now that lot had started rattling their sabres again. Someone should have drowned that Hitler at birth.

"I'll wish you a Happy Christmas. I'll see you both when I come back. You can tell me all your news then. I've got to get on my way." She pushed her chair back in and walked into the back hall.

"Happy Christmas, Mrs Acers!" the girls chorused after her.

Peggy turned back to Krista. "What are you going to

do with all your free time?" She was grateful Krista was here to see to the tradespeople. Handing out money like some kind of Lady Muck made her feel uncomfortable. She'd do it mind, when she had to, but she preferred someone else take care of that sort of thing.

"I want to see what the family have stored in the attic." She laughed when Peggy gasped in horror. The place was an insult to Peggy's idea of cleanliness and order. "I asked Lia if I might. There may well be treasure we can use up there." If there were items of sentiment or value in the attic they should be moved to a safer location – in her humble opinion.

"In the name of God, girl! Have you lost the run of your senses? There is stuff up there from before the Caulfields moved in here. It's been in Mr Caulfield's family for generations. The Lord alone knows what is up there. Why are you putting ideas in the missus' head? I don't want to be asked to clean that place out. It's so dark and dusty up there I wouldn't be surprised to find bodies buried in those deep chests."

"Think of the adventure, Peggy." Krista laughed to see the other girl's horror.

"You've lost the little sense you have." Peggy stood. "I want no part of it."

# Chapter 4

"Krista, in the name of God will you get down out of there!" Peggy stood at the foot of the ladder leading up to the attic space. "I don't know what you were thinking of going up there when you knew there was no one in the house. What if you had fallen or put your foot through ceiling or something?"

"Hello, Peggy." Krista sat on the lip of the attic opening, swinging her legs. "Did you have a nice time with your family?"

Peggy had left the day before – Christmas Day – burdened down with the gifts she had bought or made for all of her family through the year. Now she was glad to be back in her secure little room downstairs. She loved her family but a little of them went a long way.

"I am not speaking to someone risking life and limb!" she said. When she couldn't find Krista downstairs, she had come looking for her. Her heart had almost stopped when she saw the ladder leading up to the open attic. What had Krista been thinking of? "Did you find any hidden treasure?"

"There are dark paintings of very stern gentlemen up here," Krista said. "I had thought to find such paintings lining the staircase walls."

"The missus had them taken down before she moved in here," Peggy remarked absentmindedly. "You need to get down out of there and get all of that dust off you." She started off down the stairs and shouted up to Krista, "*Close that place up when you come down! I don't want all that dust around the place!*"

Krista wiggled out of the attic and stood on the small platform at the top of the A-shaped folding wooden ladder. She had to step down several rungs before she could replace the cover over the attic opening. When she had locked it into place, she climbed down until she reached the landing. She closed the ladder before wrestling it over to the tall supply cupboard standing off to one side of the landing and placing it carefully inside. She locked the door of the cupboard, hanging the key on the hook placed high to keep it out of the way of curious little boys. She wiped her hands one against the other and gave a nod of her head at a chore completed.

In the bathroom she washed her face and hands and used a clothes brush to remove the dust from her jumper and slacks. She wished she'd had longer in the attic to really look around. They had been so busy in the days since the family left. First the chimneysweep had cleaned all of the fires in the house. They had to cover all of the furniture in dust sheets before his visit. Then the window cleaners had worked on all of the windows inside and out. What she had thought would be a relaxing time was actually busier than usual with tradesmen coming and going.

The telephone in the entry hall began to ring as Krista went down the stairs. Who would be telephoning when the family was away from home? She heard Peggy answer.

"*A Mr Brown wishes to speak with you!*" Peggy walked to the bottom of the stairs to call out in her best posh voice.

Krista felt her stomach sink. Mr Brown – the Grey Man? She ran down the stairs and picked up the handset.

"Good morning, Krista here," she said, keeping the nervous tremor out of her voice with difficulty.

"I'll put the kettle on," Peggy whispered.

"Miss Lestrange?" a female voice enquired.

"Speaking,"

"I am connecting you to Mr Brown, please hold."

"Miss Lestrange," a male voice said. "We have met."

"Indeed." She recognised the voice, glad not to be under his piercing stare. The man had the police call to the house and deliver her to him at New Scotland Yard. How could she possibly forget him?

"I wish to speak with you – not over the telephone line – do you have pen and paper to hand?" Clarence

34

Brownlow-Hastings, the man calling himself Mr Brown, demanded.

"One moment." She opened the drawer in the table the telephone stood on and removed one of the pencils and notepads stored there. She opened the notepad and, with pencil at the ready, said, "You may proceed."

"Do you know Claridge's Hotel in Brooke Street?"

"Yes." She knew the large luxury red-brick hotel with its uniformed doormen. She walked past it frequently with the boys. It was almost directly across the park from the Caulfield residence.

"I have booked a table at Claridge's for afternoon tea. Four o'clock. I will send a car for you. Be prepared – and wear a skirt – we will have none of those slacks you seem so inordinately fond of."

Krista felt a shiver run down her spine. How did the man know that she wore slacks most days? They were ideal for someone running after two active young boys.

"I am afraid I am unable to comply." Krista was determined not to jump to it every time this man spoke. She had her British passport now. He had no more power over her. Besides, she needed to bathe and wash her hair. She wouldn't dare step through the intimidating grand entrance of that hotel without grooming herself to within an inch of her life.

"Nonsense, the family you are employed by are away from home. I will accept no excuses. I will send a car for you. It's just a few minutes' journey from where you are. You can postpone any plans you may have until I have spoken with you. My driver will collect you from the Caulfield house. I strongly suggest you be ready when he arrives. There are those of us who know who and what you are. You will not enjoy the consequence of defying me." He hung up the telephone.

"The nerve of the man!" Krista stood with the telephone in her hand for a moment. She slammed down the receiver and spun away. She almost ran into the kitchen. "I'll have that tea now please, Peggy!"

"What put your panties in a pucker?" Peggy poured tea into two cups.

"I have been ordered to present myself for afternoon tea at Claridge's Hotel." Krista accepted the tea with gratitude. She had been eating dust in that attic.

"*No!*" Peggy almost let the teapot drop. "Claridge's, *ooh*, that's posh! You are coming up in the world, my girl. Are you meeting Perry there? I'd be afraid of my life to put a foot inside that place. Have you seen the sour pusses on them doormen? You would think they owned the road the way they glare at people passing by." She gulped her tea, looking at Krista with sparkling eyes. "Be sure and take in everything about the place. I'll want full details from you when you get back. Imagine!" She heaved a heavy sigh. "Afternoon tea at Claridge's!"

"Will you help me decide what to wear?" Krista wasn't going to mention the Grey Man. She'd let Peggy believe she was meeting Perry. It saved detailed explanations. Something she did not have!

"Of course I will." Peggy walked into the pantry. She was hungry. She hadn't wanted to use up her mother's supply of food while she was home. Lord knows she had enough mouths to feed. "Have you had anything to eat this morning?" she called out to where Krista sat at the kitchen table.

"I had toast and the last of the eggs."

"The egg man will be calling today."

Krista was in a slight daze. What could the Grey Man want of her? And he had known what she wore when tending to the children. Why on earth would he be keeping watch on her?

Peggy stared at the abundance before her. It was always the same when she came back to the house after visiting home. Her mam had so little to share out with so many yet here there was full and plenty. It wasn't right. She didn't begrudge the family their wealth but it was wrong that so few had so much. Ah well, she couldn't solve the problems of the world standing here.

"I'm going to make myself some cheese on toast, would you like some?"

"Yes, please," Krista looked at the kitchen clock. It was just after eleven. She had hours yet to prepare herself.

"You don't want to eat too much." Peggy walked out of the pantry carrying a wheel of cheese and a cloth-wrapped loaf of bread. "I hear the food at the Claridge's Hotel is mouth-watering. You want to leave space."

The two girls busied themselves getting the snack made and served. Krista was watching Peggy out of the corner of her eye. The other girl seemed sad.

When they were both seated with tea and a snack in front of them she asked, "How was everything at home? Did they enjoy your gifts?"

"The little ones loved the gloves and socks we knit

them." Peggy had to clear her mouth of food before she could speak.

"*We* knit them!" Krista laughed. "I merely sewed the pieces together. You did all of the work."

"True, if there was a prize for tying knots in yarn you would win it every time."

"What's wrong, Peggy?" It seemed to her that Peggy was trying to be cheerful.

"There were ructions in the house." Peggy shoved the last of the bread she held into her mouth. "Three of me brothers were talking about war coming. They said they are going to join up before they are called up. Honest to God, Krista, you would think they were talking about going on a foreign holiday. Me mam boxed their ears and called them 'stupid cannon fodder'." She closed her eyes briefly. "It didn't make for a happy holiday, I can tell you."

"I'm sorry, Peggy." Krista didn't know what else to say. She imagined a great many families across the land had the same kind of discussion over the Christmas meal.

"Yes, so am I." Peggy dreaded to think of her brothers going to war but there was little she could do to prevent them. They were grown men, most of them. "So, let's talk about something more cheerful – Claridge's." She waved her hand at Krista, determined to keep her spirits up. "Who would have thought it?"

"A car is being sent for me." Krista was willing to change the subject. "It will be here just before four. It's just a few minutes' journey by car apparently."

"Then what are you doing sitting in the kitchen?"

Peggy snapped. "Get upstairs and wash. You're wearing half the dirt from the attic in your hair and on your skin. Move it, missus. We have to get you cocked, powdered and shaved before you'll be fit to be seen." She almost pulled Krista from her seat. "This is so exciting. Imagine – Claridge's!"

"I'm glad one of us is excited." Krista allowed herself to be pushed from the kitchen.

"Do you think you should borrow a fur coat from the missus?" Peggy said from outside the bathroom door.

"What are you talking about?" Krista was on her knees in the bath pouring hot water over her head using the plastic jug kept in the bathroom for that purpose.

"If you're going to swank it into Claridge's you should wear one of the furs the missus keeps in her closet. I'm sure she wouldn't mind." Peggy could imagine Krista wrapped in the fox-fur full-length coat that she'd been admiring for years.

"I'll wear my red swing coat, thank you very much!" She worked shampoo into her hair. "You are getting above yourself, Peggy Matthews."

"Listen to you." Peggy laughed. Krista's English language skills were impressive. She understood the everyday English that Peggy and Mrs Acers spoke well enough but when she spoke she sounded to the life like one of those ones off the wireless. "We need to make you gorgeous. I'm taking your shoes and bag down to the scullery to give them a polish. Give us a shout when you're ready for them. I've put the hair-drying machine in your bedroom. You don't want to be going into Claridge's with wet hair. Besides, you'd catch your death of cold."

"What would I do without you, Peggy?" Krista rinsed the shampoo out of her hair, trying not to laugh and get a mouthful of soapy water.

"Look at you!" Peggy admired the image Krista presented. "It's a shame we didn't take a photograph of you before and after." She laughed.

"Do I look like someone who would sashay her way into Claridge's?" Krista was standing in front of the mirror in the entry hallway, arranging the red hat that matched her coat. Her stomach was awash with nervous butterflies.

"You look lovely," Peggy reassured her. "Perry won't be able to take his eyes off you."

"That must be the car." Krista heard the sound of brakes being applied outside the house. She turned to open the door but Peggy stopped her with a hand on her arm.

"It is my job to open the door." She pushed Krista gently back towards the drawing-room entrance. "You don't want to appear too eager – wait until the driver knocks."

Krista walked into the drawing room, the navy skirt of the waisted dress she wore under her hip-length swing coat swaying around her silk-stockinged legs. She pressed a hand to her stomach, desperately afraid she would throw up. What could the Grey Man want of her? She waited nervously, listening to Peggy greet the driver of the car.

"The car is here, miss." Peggy stood in the open doorway of the drawing room, a huge grin on her face. With her back to the hallway the driver wouldn't see the wink she gave Krista.

"Thank you, Peggy." Krista walked out into the hallway, her head held high. She took her navy leather clutch bag and gloves from the hallway hatstand and walked out of the house and down the walkway to where the driver stood holding open the rear door of a luxury model car. She folded her long body onto the rear butter-soft seats, trying to gather her composure. It would not do to present a weak front to the driver. She had the notion that the Grey Man would demand a report on her behaviour from him.

"It is just a short journey, Miss Lestrange," the driver said when he'd taken his seat behind the wheel.

"Thank you." She tried to enjoy the greenery of the park as they drove across its width. When they reached the hotel, she waited until the hotel doorman had rushed forward to open her car door. She gave a nod of thanks to the doorman as she stepped out, and with a deep breath prepared to step into one of London's most luxurious hotels.

# Chapter 5

The foyer of the hotel was stunning. The black and white tiles lit by glowing crystal chandeliers took her breath away. It was all a visual delight. She would have to remember details to share with Peggy. There was a roaring fire off to one side with leather chairs placed invitingly in front of it. She thought she would wait there for the Grey Man. Before she could move, however, she noticed a smartly dressed man walking towards her.

"Miss Lestrange." The man stepped up to Krista's side. "Barlow, assistant manager. Mr Brown is waiting for you. If you would follow me?" He indicated an entryway off the lobby.

The sound of chatter and laughter coming from the

room he indicated sounded delightful. In other circumstances she would be thrilled with being in this hotel. She would love the chance to look around.

"Thank you." Krista tried not to appear gauche.

Clarence Brownlow-Hastings watched the hotel manager lead the young woman through the wide aisle between tables to where he waited. He had deliberately asked for a table placed deep into the large room elegantly set up for the serving of afternoon tea. He wanted to judge this young woman who interested him. She did not look out of place. She appeared to be taking the grandeur of the hotel in her stride. It was a far cry from the little *auberge* she'd been raised in! He stood at her approach.

"Mr Brown." Krista unbuttoned her coat but didn't remove it. She placed her small clutch bag and gloves carefully on the white linen-covered tabletop.

The table had been set for tea for two with delightful china crockery and silverware, and everything sparkled.

Barlow clicked his fingers at a waiter standing almost to attention by a serving table close to one wall. The man hurried forward.

"Take the lady's coat," the assistant manager ordered.

"Thank you." Krista allowed the coat to fall from her shoulders into the waiter's hands. She didn't turn to look as the waiter hurried away.

Barlow pulled out the seat across from Brown, holding its back while he waited for her to sit.

"Miss Lestrange, thank you for joining me." Brown continued to stand, amused at the glare from those beautiful blue eyes.

Krista allowed Barlow to seat her and push the chair closer to the table. She prayed she wouldn't hit the table with her knees.

"Do let me know if there is anything I can help you with." Barlow prepared to leave. He knew the man calling himself Brown. He mentally shrugged. It wasn't his job to wonder about the behaviour of their guests.

"Thank you." Krista never removed her eyes from Brown as he sat down but she was aware of Barlow departing with silent grace.

"Why have you summoned me here?" Krista asked immediately.

"Summoned? My dear Miss Lestrange!" Clarence smiled. "I invited a charming lady to join me for afternoon tea."

"I was given no opportunity to refuse your invitation!" Krista snapped.

"Miss Lestrange …"

Before he could comment further a waiter stepped up to the table with large menus. The discussion as to the type of tea desired was long and detailed. The sommelier at the Auberge du Ville didn't discuss the choice of wine to have with your meal in such detail. Krista felt she could have gone to India and picked the tea leaves, the two men spoke so long about the tea. She waited patiently, having nothing to add to the discussion. She was far from being a tea expert, for goodness' sake. When they began to discuss the sandwiches on offer, she almost rolled her eyes.

While the men spoke, she examined the others in the room. They were predominately women dressed in the height of fashion, with fur stoles draped around their shoulders. She listened to the muted conversations around her, enjoying earwigging as Peggy would call it. There was no talk of war or personal problems. The conversations seemed to deal primarily with fashion and with gossip about people in their social set. She would have to share every little detail with Mrs Acers and Peggy. This was a far cry from a pot of tea in the kitchen.

She settled back to enjoy the experience. It would seem afternoon tea was a serious business!

"May I say you look delightful, Miss Lestrange," Clarence said as soon as the waiter had taken his order and left. He had been aware of her interest in the room and the people surrounding them. She had been discreet but she had been taking in the happenings around them. That boded well for the future.

"Thank you," Krista almost bit out between clenched teeth. This man wanted something from her – being charming to her wouldn't relax her guard. She waited for him to speak. After all, he had demanded her presence here – he could tell her what he wanted of her while she enjoyed this experience.

"Captain Waters assures me you conducted yourself on his mission with skill and diplomacy." Clarence saw their waiter pushing a trolley towards their table. He spread his white linen napkin over his lap, waiting for her to speak. When she remained silent, he smiled to himself. Better and better.

The waiter stopped with the trolley to the right of Krista. With white gloved hands, he placed a laden silver cake stand on the table, followed by a large silver teapot and another silver pot. Then he turned the brightly patterned china cups on the table upright on their matching saucers.

He gestured towards the large silver teapot on the trolley. "Darjeeling as requested," he said softly. "Hot water if required." He gestured again towards the smaller of the two silver pots. "Shall I serve?"

"Thank you, no." Clarence waved a dismissal. "We will serve ourselves."

"As you wish." The waiter half bowed, and turned to leave. "Enjoy your tea."

"Will you be Mother, my dear?" Clarence said.

"I beg your pardon?" Krista was confused.

"It is an English expression. It simply means to take charge of serving the tea to the requirements of your guests. You'd do well to learn our expressions. You do not want to appear foreign – not at this moment in time in England."

"I make no claim to be English." Krista reached for the ivory handle of the large silver teapot. She had observed Lia serving her friends afternoon tea many times. She had passed around the cups and dainties to her guests before taking her seat and joining in the conversation. This was the first time she would be responsible for actually serving the tea. She hoped the deep breath she took to steady her nerves was not apparent to the eagle-eyed man across the table from her. It would be a disgrace to have the cup she picked up rattle in its saucer. She poured the tea elegantly as she'd seen Lia do, pleased with herself. "Milk?"

"Never with Darjeeling, my dear – lemon." Clarence enjoyed her grace and poise as he watched her every movement. Yes, indeed, breeding would out – no one would ever know she had been a serving wench in some dreadful out-of-the-way French *auberge*.

Krista continued to serve the man across the table from her, gritting her teeth as she offered him a selection of dainty sandwiches from the bottom tier of the serving trolley. They indulged in excruciatingly polite conversation. They discussed the weather – frightful. The holiday season – joyful. The Caulfield children – delightful. The happenings in Europe – dreadful. By the time they had partaken of the scones with cream and jam and reached the cakes on the top tier of the stand, Krista was ready to scream. The man watched her every move. She felt as if she was being visually dissected. What did he want of her?

"Mr Grey …" She cringed at her faux pas.

"Brown."

"As you say." Her raised eyebrow let him know she didn't believe for a moment that Brown was his name. She refused to apologise for calling him by the wrong colour. She popped one of the tiny bite-sized cakes into her mouth and chewed slowly. The pastry chef at this hotel must be a Frenchman, she thought as she enjoyed the flavour. "Mr Brown, you demanded my presence here." She looked around the tearoom for a moment. "Perhaps you would be good enough to tell me why?"

"You were gifted designer clothing when you agreed to work for Captain Waters." Clarence blotted his lips with his napkin and waited. She really was delightful. She could converse on inane subjects – served tea to the manner born – yet didn't sink meekly into the background. Yes, indeed. He could use her. "Were you not?" he prompted when she remained silent.

"You appear to know a great deal about my life, Mr Brown," Krista said. "I believe you know the answer to that question as well as I."

"Indeed." He was positively delighted with her. Not many young women or indeed men could stand up under his glare. "I wish you to answer nonetheless."

"I was gifted a number of items – yes." Krista was wearing one of the outfits from those designer items – which must be apparent to this man who seemed to see so much.

"Good – good." Clarence carefully blotted his lips. He looked around the room, moving only his eyes. No one appeared to be paying any attention to them, each table involved in discussion. "Our European brethren do not appear to celebrate Christmas in quite the same way as we British do ... " He paused a moment, wondering if she would say anything. "It would appear the New Year is the time of great celebration to those outside these shores ... " Still no response. She knew how to wait. Good! "I have a duty for you to perform ... I wish you to attend a number of celebrations at a selection of the many foreign embassies in London. I will supply a list of the gentlemen you will accompany." He sat back and waited.

"The clothing I received was not at all suitable for attending Embassy balls." Krista was almost weak with relief that she could refuse without causing offence.

"We have your measurements." He waved away her objection. "It will be a simple matter to find you suitable clothing." He knew a number of the better design houses kept partially assembled garments in case of emergency. The girl opposite him had the same measurements as the models the design showrooms employed. One of his men had made mention of that fact.

"I am at a loss as to what you require of me," Krista said.

"It is a simple matter. I wish you to employ your language skills and obvious charms to ingratiate yourself to the higher level of staff at these balls. You will report anything you may hear to me – and only me." Who would suspect her of intelligence if she batted those big blue eyes in his direction? Add in the abundance of alcohol at these events and heaven alone knew what might be discovered!

"Let me see if I understand." Krista leaned forward and almost hissed. "You wish me to accompany a number of gentlemen unknown to me to evenings of celebration at foreign embassies and spend my time flirting with them while I try to discover any and all secrets floating in the air?"

"Exactly."

"*No.*"

"Why on earth would you refuse?" Clarence had not expected this. Was it not every poor girl's dream to 'go to the ball'?

"You wish me to become known as a floozy, Mr Brown?" Krista felt her flesh crawl. How dare this man try to turn her into his informant!

"Not at all!"

"Mr Brown ..." Krista looked for the waiter. She

wanted her coat. She was leaving. "Mata Hari may be portrayed as a seductive and dangerous war spy in popular books and films these days. We in Europe know the truth."

"But ... but ..." Clarence spluttered. How on earth had he lost control of this conversation?

"I will not be your spy, Mr Brown." Krista removed the linen napkin from her lap and threw it on the table. "I will not destroy my reputation to fulfil some self-seeking power game that you appear to be playing. I am leaving – thank you for the tea." She stood, pushing her chair back.

Clarence was forced to stand or appear unforgivably rude. He grabbed one of her elbows before she could storm out. "Young lady ... I never ..."

Krista refused to allow him to continue.

"I have always found it fascinating that both of the men – French and German – that used Margaretha Geertruida Zelle McLeod AKA Mata Hari for their own purposes escaped with a rap on the knuckles and promotions, while the unfortunate woman they blackmailed into spying for them was taken before a firing squad and shot! There is a lesson in there for all women, don't you think, Mr Brown?" She pulled her arm free and raised a hand to summon a waiter and ask for her coat.

# Chapter 6

Krista failed to storm out of the tearoom as she wished. The waiter and Brown politely insisted she wait while the remains of the afternoon tea were boxed up. The tea trolley was taken from the table. Brown almost smirked when he explained to her that it was a tradition of the hotel to box up the leftovers for the enjoyment of household staff.

They sat in uncomfortable silence as they waited. Krista used the time to make mental note of all she wanted to share with Peggy and Mrs Acers.

She almost sighed with relief when the waiter returned with her coat over his arm and two pretty white boxes tied with bright scarlet ribbons. He helped her into her coat before presenting the two white boxes to her with a bow. With a regal nod to Brown who had stood up with her, she put her clutch bag under her arm, pulled on her gloves, put two fingers through the ribbon loops on the boxes and left the hotel with her head held high and as much dignity as she could muster.

She struggled one-handed to pull the deep collar of her swing coat up around her ears. It was a cold, grey, miserable day. She felt the mucky water from the puddles on the path through the park land on the back of her legs. She could feel the chill through her silk stockings. She muttered dire warnings to the Grey Man as she thought of Brown under her breath. The bright red of her coat and hat was a splash of colour in the green and brown of her surroundings. She marched along, looking neither to the right or left, simply wanting to get home and out of these clothes that were in no way suitable for outdoor pursuits in an English winter.

"I should have worn my waterproof outfit to meet that man," she muttered into the collar of her coat. "It would serve him right if I had made a holy show of him as Peggy would say." She fought the tears that wanted to fall, unsure if she was sad or angry. How dare that man think to turn her into a floozy! Had he no clue of the gossip that circulated in society? It would only take one woman seeing her twice on the arms of different men and her name would be mud. Lia had warned her repeatedly of the catty women that entertained themselves with malicious gossip. She did not belong in that society and had no wish to!

*"Kris, will you wait up!"*

A hand on her elbow halting her caused her to swing around with a clenched fist, ready to defend herself.

"Perry!" she gasped. "Where did you come from?"

"Did you not hear me calling you? I want to speak with you. I called to the Caulfield house." Perry fell into step beside her. "Imagine my surprise when Peggy informed me that you had gone to meet me for afternoon tea at Claridge's! I pretended I had misunderstood our arrangement." He had set out to meet her at the hotel. He had not expected to encounter her in the park. The sight of her familiar bright-red coat and hat had shone out in the dark park like a beacon.

Krista offered no explanation. Men were not her favourite species right at this moment. She continued her quick march along the path leading towards the Caulfield house. Perry matched her step, his longer legs and silver-headed walking stick helping him to easily keep pace.

"Allow me to carry your boxes," he offered, wondering who had put that look on Krista's face. He had hoped to appeal to her good nature but someone else had obviously just abused that very nature. He could not let that deter him. He needed her help and advice.

"Thank you." She passed the boxes to him. "I want to get in out of this weather."

She couldn't refuse to speak with him. She was curious as to why he had sought her out. She wanted to sigh and hang her head. The life she was living confused her. She was an employee of the Caulfield family. She felt uneasy inviting guests into a house that was not her home. Lia had told her repeatedly that she should make the house her own, but how could she?

"I have to change out of this outfit," she said as they approached the Caulfield house. "You may wait in the kitchen with Peggy."

She wanted to laugh at the shock on his face. Perry was not a man accustomed to sitting waiting in someone's kitchen. He expected to sit in the drawing room with his feet to the fire, being waited on hand and foot. Well, tough. He could keep Peggy company. He might learn a little about how the other half lived.

They walked in silence until they reached the entryway to the Caulfield house. Krista's sigh of relief almost shook the collar of her coat, it was so deep and heartfelt. She took the key to the door from her small purse and hurried to open the door and get inside. As soon as she had the door partially open, she shouted for Peggy.

"*In the name of all that's holy –*" Peggy appeared in the open door of the kitchen, a scowl on her face. "Oh, sir ... I-I didn't know you were there," she stuttered.

"Perry, if you would pass those boxes to Peggy." Krista was walking towards the stairs as she spoke. "You may hang your hat and coat on the hallstand. Peggy, please take him into the kitchen. I simply must get out of this outfit and into something warm. I will join you shortly."

"*The kitchen!*" Peggy took the two boxes Perry almost pushed into her hands.

Krista didn't answer as she was halfway up the stairs. Perry had called unexpectedly. He could take them as he found them.

"It would appear we have our orders." Perry smiled into the maid's shocked face. "If you would lead the way?"

"I don't know what the world's coming to – I really don't," Peggy muttered as she led the way to the kitchen. Still, it was the warmest room in the house. She put the two boxes on the table, wondering what was in them. "If she wants any of that coffee she drinks, she can make it herself. She moans that I don't make it properly." She turned to Perry, hoping she was masking how uncomfortable she felt. "Would you like a pot of tea?" She hoped he would say yes. It would give her something to do with her hands.

"Thank you but let's wait for Krista."

While Peggy was in the kitchen, mentally cursing her, the woman herself was upstairs groaning at the mess that decorated the back of her legs. The dark-brown mud splashes would have to be washed out of her silk stockings and off her legs. She had hoped to take the time to calm down and think about the meeting with Brown. With Perry downstairs that option was no longer open to her. She undressed swiftly, checking the back of her dress for mud splashes. She shook her head at the mess she had made of herself – pride came before a fall – she should have taken a taxi.

"Perry, you will have to wait while I warm up," Krista said as she opened the kitchen door, interrupting the awkward conversation Perry was trying to conduct with Peggy. "Those bedrooms are like ice-boxes." She took long-legged strides across the kitchen floor, glad to be once more wearing slacks. The brown tweed slacks, thick socks and heavy handknit sweater were warm but she needed something more to combat the chill the day had left on her body. She opened the door covering the range fire and stood basking in the warmth.

"You should open those boxes, Peggy." Krista looked over her shoulder and jerked her chin towards the two boxes sitting unopened on the table between her two companions. "We can have a feast."

"I thought you just had afternoon tea?" Peggy pushed back her chair, glad of something to do.

"As far as I could see, Peggy, people go to that fancy place to be seen. They nibble on the food. They don't eat."

"*Oooh*, look at those pretty sandwiches!" Peggy had opened one of the boxes. "Brown and white bread – fancy! And such lovely little scones!" She opened the second box and almost swooned at the gorgeous cakes inside. "I'll get something to put these on." She hurried out of the kitchen and into the dining room to fetch the silver platters. She wasn't going to put those fancy sandwiches and cakes on china plates. Not with a member of the gentry present.

"So, Perry," Krista carefully closed the door to the range fire before joining Perry at the kitchen table, "I think my bones have defrosted now. What can I do for you?"

"My mother wishes to meet you."

Peggy arrived back with the silver platters and began to arrange the sandwiches on one of them.

"Does she – why?" Krista asked.

"Mother …" He glanced at Peggy and paused.

"Peggy wouldn't dream of discussing anything she hears here," Krista said.

"Did you not know that staff are trained to be selectively deaf?" Peggy put the first of the silver salvers on the table.

"Thank you, Peggy." Perry smiled. "I am having great difficulty handling the changes that are taking place in my world." So many things he thought he knew were proving to be false. The last months had been eye-opening for him.

"With the news coming out of that wireless, I believe we will all be learning new ways soon." Peggy busied herself arranging the cakes, her mouth watering in anticipation of that first bite. She hoped they tasted as good as they looked!

"Your mother, Perry?" Krista prompted before they became involved in a discussion of world events.

"Captain Waters, my mother and our instructors are tearing their hair out at the difficulty of impressing the need for foreign language skills on the members of my group." Perry spoke as Peggy busied herself setting up the table for what she liked to think of as a posh tea. "We are the first, Krista, and we are failing miserably."

"I don't understand the problem." Krista had been tested in her own language skills by Captain Waters. The captain spoke English, French and German fluently as he'd proved while testing her. "Surely your group must contain people who speak more than one language? Would that not have been a part of the selection process?"

"One would have thought so," Perry shook his head sadly, "but no."

"Are they all Hurrah Henrys like you?" Peggy put pretty china cups and saucers on the tabletop. She almost laughed aloud at the shocked look on Perry's face. Well, what did he expect? He was talking in front of her and she had a mouth and an opinion, didn't she?

"Do you really think of me as a Hurrah Henry, Peggy? I am shocked." Perry laughed.

"What is a Hurrah Henry?" Krista didn't understand the term.

"People like Perry here." Peggy continued to set the table while waiting for the pot of tea she'd made to brew. "Young men who were born with a silver spoon in their mouths and haven't the first clue about real life. They swan around town enjoying the best of everything – never a worry in their little heads."

"Peggy, I am hurt." Perry put a hand to his chest and gave the two young women a sad look. Perhaps he had been a Hurrah Henry once upon a time but no more. His accident had forced him to face reality.

"But is she right?" Krista asked.

"I really hadn't given it any thought," Perry said, "but upon reflection I am forced to admit you may be right, Peggy." He would have to share this opinion with his mother. Were they doomed to failure almost before they'd begun because of their failure to select the right type of men?

"All of the people chosen for this course of study are male?" Krista waited for his nod before saying, "That was very short-sighted of someone."

"My mother agrees and has said so rather forcefully upon occasion. That is why she wishes to meet with you, Krista."

"What has your mother to do with the course and students?" Krista accepted a cup of tea from Peggy.

"I believe I have made mention of my shock when I

discovered my own mother had been part of naval intelligence in the Great War?" Perry had shared his bewilderment upon his discovery of his mother's role in the Great War with Krista.

"You did," Krista said as Peggy sat down at the table with them.

"My mother and a select group of people including Captain Waters are frustrated with the powers that be." Perry accepted a sandwich from the platter Peggy held out to him. "They appear to believe that should there be another war it will follow the same path as the Great War – they are planning for trench warfare, for heaven's sake."

"What has any of that to do with Krista?" Peggy tried not to gulp down the little sandwich she'd selected. It was delicious. She'd never tasted anything like it. She wanted to open the sandwich and have a good look at its contents but didn't want to appear ignorant before Perry. "She can hardly be expected to go up to the powers that be and bang their heads together. Although there are a few I could name that need their ears boxed."

"Wouldn't that be wonderful?" Perry threw his head back and laughed.

"What does your mother expect of me?" Krista asked.

"Mother has plans for you she hasn't shared with me. I only know Mother hopes to secure your assistance."

# Chapter 7

Krista pulled one of the two easy chairs kept tucked away in the boot room – an out-of-the-way large dark room off the kitchen – towards the range. She'd already added coal to the range fire. The two chairs were kept for the rare occasions staff could sit at their ease. She was wearing heavy men's pyjamas and a robe. She had planned to fill a hot-water bottle and take it up to bed with her but the silence and welcoming heat of the kitchen had tempted her to remain.

She opened the door of the range to uncover the blazing fire inside. She kicked off her fleece-lined leather slippers, curling her legs up onto the seat of the wide soft chair. She stared into the flames of the fire, practically begging the wheels in her mind to stop turning. She wanted to sleep – wanted this day to be over. Peggy was with her family. She'd had to almost push the young woman out the door. She wanted, no needed, to be alone.

New Year's Eve – the last day of the year. If she had remained in France with the Dumas family – at this time of this day – she would have been exhausted but unable to seek her bed until the last of the drunken revellers left the bar/tabac. She wondered where Philippe Dumas was spending this evening. She hoped he was in good company enjoying himself. Philippe, the young man she thought was her brother. Philippe, the one who had informed her she was no relation of the Dumas family. He had set her free with his words, did he but know it. Philippe had run away from his family, unable to fight their support of Hitler and his bully boys. He had fled the *auberge* only hours before Krista had been forced to flee. Had he found people to help him?

New Year's Eve, she supposed, was a time of reflection. Time to think of the year past and plan for the year ahead. She bit back a sob. She was not feeling sorry for herself. She was frightened. What would the coming year, 1939, hold for her? She had changed her life by running away from the Dumas family – from her life of servitude at the Auberge du Ville. She had found help, people who seemed to want to assist her. Was it ungrateful of her to resent that some of the people she had met wanted to use her?

There had been no mention made of paying her by Brown or Perry. The money Lia Caulfield paid her was a small amount and could be considered pin money. It was very difficult for a single woman to earn enough to support herself. It was all very well for people who had family money behind them to volunteer their services but she needed to support herself. She couldn't live on fresh air. Captain Waters had paid her generously for her journey into Germany. That money was in the Post Office and knowing she had some funds behind her was a source of great comfort to her. But, as Violet said, you only got to have money if you didn't spend it! She had to have a source of income before she could step away from the safe little cocoon the friends she had made in this country had found for her.

She sat in silent reflection for a time, staring into the flames making pictures out of the sparks and smoke that rose from the burning coals.

"I am making myself thoroughly miserable." She unfolded her long legs, pushing her feet into her slippers. "I have nothing to moan about."

She moved around the space that had become so familiar to her over the past seven – almost eight – months. She took the jug of milk out of the cold box and with practised movements began to assemble what she needed to make a mug of hot chocolate. She continued to speak aloud. The gentle sound of the language of her own country comforted her. She began to unconsciously count her blessings.

"I have a comfortable roof over my head. There is always food available to me. I can make a fire whenever I want. The Caulfield family treat me well. What more do I need, for goodness' sake?" She kept an eye on the milk in the little pot on top of the range while looking around the large kitchen with a smile. She'd never had anywhere this comfortable to rant and rave before. In the past her little room under the eaves of the *auberge* had been the only space that felt like hers. She had frozen in winter in that room and baked in summer.

"The Grey Man wants to use me." She moved the little pot of hot milk to a cooler part of the range. Talking away to herself, she went into the pantry in search of the block of cooking chocolate. "It sounds to me as if Perry and his mother want to use me too." She took the chocolate, wrapped in waxed paper and covered in a muslin cloth, from deep at the back of a shelf. She continued to chat away to herself as she grated the chocolate into the milk. She returned the chocolate to the pantry before moving the pot over the hottest part of the range again, stirring briskly with a whisk as she waited for the chocolate to melt into the liquid.

"I am alone."

She poured the liquid into a heavy china mug she'd had close to hand. She put the pot in to soak in the big white butler's sink before sitting back down in the easy chair. She took a sip of her drink, staring once more into the fire.

"It is strange. I have always felt alone – even when I was surrounded by the Dumas family – I felt separated from them. I thought it was because I was the lone female after three sons. It was a relief to discover that I was no relation to any of them. Still ..."

She put her mug on top of the range, well out of the way of the hottest part. She stood and walked over to the kitchen wireless. The BBC were broadcasting a concert from the Savoy Hotel ballroom. She needed music to keep her company. She played with the round dials of the wireless until she found the programme she wanted. When the music began to fill the room she raised her arms and, with her eyes shut, began to waltz around the empty kitchen. She was unaware of the tears flowing from her eyes, lost in her dream world. The music continued to play as she spun alone in the empty house.

"Oh, thank you, sweet baby Jesus!" Peggy almost exploded into the kitchen. "I was praying you wouldn't be in bed, Krista, and the kitchen fire out. I am blue with the cold."

"Peggy!" Krista stared at her friend from her seat before the fire. The music from the wireless no longer played. The concert had ended when the New Year was played in. "I thought you would spend the night at your home."

"Be a love, Krista, and pull the other chair out." Peggy was busy unwrapping herself. She had so many layers of clothing on she felt like an overstuffed sausage. "I am cold to the marrow of my bones." She shrugged out of her heavy tweed coat, pushing her hat and gloves into one of the coat sleeves. "I want to sit in peace and quiet for a minute. I'll make us both hot-water bottles to take to bed with us."

"Should I make you a mug of hot chocolate?" Krista asked as she began to push the second easy chair close to the range.

"Ta but no." Peggy, after throwing her outer garments into her room off the kitchen, hurried to lend a hand. "I am awash in liquid. In our house we don't sing in the New Year. We drown the Old Year in booze."

Krista hadn't a notion what Peggy meant but she didn't ask her to explain. She was so glad to be no longer alone with the big house echoing around her.

"Did you enjoy your evening?" Krista asked when both women were settled before the fire.

Peggy didn't answer at once but continued to stare into the flames. She turned to look at Krista, a deep sigh shaking her slim body.

"My mother said that working here has given me ideas above my station."

"Why?" Krista prompted when Peggy said no more.

"I love my family. I really do." Peggy almost sobbed. "But I don't want what my mother has. I don't want to be a slave to a man and have a baby every year. My mother called me an unnatural woman tonight. We had a big row. She wants me to start walking out with Billy Porter, the local butcher. Krista, the man is old and fat. He has buried two wives and has a slew of snotnosed children. His children from his first wife are older than me. I won't do it!" Peggy wailed.

Krista jumped out of her chair. She opened a drawer in the kitchen cupboard and pulled out a tea towel. She hurried over to sit on the arm of Peggy's chair, putting her arm around the other girl as she sobbed. She pushed the tea towel into her hands to give her something to wipe her face with. The only sound in the kitchen was the heart-breaking sobs that shook Peggy's body.

"I'm sorry," Peggy said huskily when her tears finally stopped. "This is no way to start the New

Year." She used the tea towel to soak up her tears and blow her nose. "I feel as if I have done nothing but shout and argue all night and now this ..." She patted the hand Krista put on her shoulder. "I am fine now." She continued to pat Krista's soft hand. "I swear."

"You should not go to bed when you are so upset." Krista stood away from Peggy's chair and took her own seat again. "You will never get to sleep." She knew all too well what it was like to lie awake staring at the ceiling while her thoughts ran around in circles.

"Do you think we are going to war?" Peggy didn't look at Krista as she asked. "That is all anyone seemed to talk about tonight. We had the whole street in and everyone talked about that man Hitler. You would think they could solve the problems of the world the way the men were talking. My own brothers were the worst of the bunch. They are still saying they are going to join the services – they want to fight for their country – *hah* – as if anyone would want them."

"Perhaps that is why your mother wishes to see you safely settled with Mr Porter the local butcher." Krista offered softly. "A butcher shop is a good business. You would never go hungry."

"Don't you start with that guff!" Peggy snapped. "I'd be dead and buried in a year living with that old goat."

"There is my friend Peggy!" Krista laughed under the glare from Peggy's eyes. "I don't like to see you weeping and wailing."

"Seriously though ..." Peggy smiled, "I want to know your answer. You know more about what is going on in Europe than that crowd of drunken boasters at my house. Do you think we will be at war next year? What am I talking about? It is already next year. This year, I mean. I can't bear to think about it but do you really believe that England will go to war?"

"Yes. I am afraid so. In my opinion England will have no option but to fight Hitler." What else could she say? Hitler would march over the world if he was not stopped.

"What are we going to do?" Peggy stared at Krista as if she held all the answers.

"I have no crystal ball, Peggy. I can't advise you, I'm afraid."

"Well, we'd better get ready for bed or we'll be no use to man nor beast today." Peggy stood. "If you push the two chairs back into place I'll make us two hot-water bottles. We can try to escape our troubles in dreamland."

# Chapter 8

"Krista!"

"Krista, did you miss me?"

David and Edward jumped out of the car, announcing their safe arrival in loud tones.

Peggy and Krista had been keeping watch for the car carrying the Caulfield family. Lia could not give them an exact time of arrival but she had telephoned the house just before the family left Captain Caulfield's family estate in Norfolk. As soon as the car was spotted turning into the square Peggy had run to tell Mrs Acers while Krista had stepped outside to wait on the black-and-white paving of the entryway. Peggy was soon back by Krista's side.

"Krista, Papa manned the lifeboat!" David rammed

his body into Krista, almost knocking her off her feet.

"We went out to sea with the fishermen!" Edward too attached himself to Krista.

"Papa had to tie us to the ship's rails," David laughed.

"In case we went overboard." Edward's grin almost split his little face.

"Hello, Peggy, Krista." Lia was not her usual immaculately groomed self. "Remind me never to leave home without both of you again." Her smile was weary. "I have been wrestling little monkeys for what seemed like an eternity."

"I will take these monkeys off your hands now, Lia," Krista said.

"Welcome home, Mrs Caulfield." Peggy hurried to open the entry door. She'd closed it behind them to keep the heat inside. She had fires burning in all the rooms to welcome the little family back home. "Mrs Acers has the kettle on."

"Boys, touch nothing until we get those hands washed." Krista was pushing the two boys towards the stairs as she spoke.

"There is a van following the car, Peggy." A weary Lia walked past Peggy into the house. "If you would show the men into the kitchen and tell Mrs Acers I am ready for a pot of tea as soon as she has it ready to serve." She pushed the hair from her face with a tired sigh.

"I'll do that, Mrs Caulfield," Peggy hurried forward to assist the driver of the car. "Hello, Mr Goleby, can I give you a hand with anything?"

"You can carry this lot in." Cyrus Goleby, a portly man with rugged weather-beaten features, opened the rear door of the car and pointed to the bags strewn around the floor. He winced at the marks on the pristine leather of the car seat. He was that glad to have reached their destination he wanted to kiss the ground. He'd been saying it for years – those two young lads would be happier taking the train home – and he'd be spared the wear and tear on his nerves watching them jump around the place.

Peggy gathered up the bags of leftover snacks and toys that had been used to try and keep the twins entertained on the long car journey. "It's nice to see you again, Mr Goleby. How's the family?"

"All is well, thank the Lord." Cyrus Goleby was a familiar figure at the London house. It was his job to collect and return the family to London whenever they visited the captain's home. "The lads are following with the van, young Peggy. See they unpack everything, would you? I'm off to the kitchen. I hope Wilma Acers has food and drink for hungry men – none of them fancy meals you women eat."

Peggy ignored his grumbling. She knew as well as he did that Mrs Acers would have a rich nourishing soup and thick sandwiches waiting for the men.

In the children's bathroom Krista was using a wet face towel to scrub the grime off the two little boys.

"Did you miss me, Krista?" David scrunched up his face against the attack of the well-soaped facecloth.

"How in the world did you get bread and butter behind your ears?" Krista held David's head steady while she tried to remove whatever was decorating his ears and in his hair. She could only imagine the twins had indulged in a wrestling match while eating.

"We missed you," Edward said when it was his turn

to be washed. "Mama was ever so busy and Grandma does not like to run around in the cold getting dirty." He scrunched up his lips and closed his eyes.

"I missed both of you."

Krista took a thick comb and tried to restore some sort of order to their black hair. Getting them truly clean would have to wait until this evening when she got them both in a hot bath and scrubbed them.

She wrapped her arms around them both. "The house was so silent without you two making noise." She pressed a noisy kiss onto each cheek then took each little boy by the hand and left the bathroom.

"We are never noisy." Edward skipped along.

"You must be thinking of some other boys," David said.

The two boys pulled their hands from Krista's, running towards the staircase.

"*Be careful, boys!*" Krista shouted. "Do not run on the stairs. It is dangerous." She rolled her eyes, knowing they would ignore her words. She ran after the two boys as they charged down the stairs and towards the family room to the rear of the house.

"Mama, Krista said that we are noisy," said David.

"My boys," Lia put her teacup down, smiling at Krista when she stepped into the room. "I think you must be mistaken, Krista."

"That is what we said." David jerked his head in agreement.

"We are good boys." Edward joined his twin by his mother's side. "Grandma calls us her little angels."

"I cannot imagine what I was thinking." Krista laughed.

The two women would have to wait to catch up with their news. It would take the two of them to exhaust the boys before bedtime.

In the kitchen Bert and Sam, the two fresh-faced young men who had driven the van to London were being ordered around by Mrs Acers. She'd had years of experience preparing her kitchen cupboards for the abundance she knew would arrive into her kitchen. It was the same every time the family returned from the country. Her kitchen became choked with goods sent from the Caulfield home farm. The geese would have to be cooked. The smoked ham stored. The vegetables and fruit would need to be stored in a dark corner of the pantry until she could make use of them.

"Young Peggy," Cyrus Goleby said as the men sat around the kitchen table enjoying hearty beef stew and sandwiches, "these two young fellow-me-lads want to see the sights of London before they return home." He nodded towards a blushing Bert, and Sam who was slurping a chunk of beef off his spoon. "I thought you might be free to show them around and keep them out of danger. They've never been to London before."

"Oh, will you not be exhausted after driving all this way?" Mrs Acers was making a large pot of tea for the men to enjoy after their meal. "You have to drive back to Norfolk tonight and be ready for your day's work tomorrow."

"They're young." Cyrus laughed softly. "It's a treat for farm lads to visit London, don't yeh know? Shame to miss seeing the sights."

"I'll have to check with Mrs Caulfield." Peggy looked at the two strapping young lads. She'd have to keep a close eye on them – see they weren't led astray. There were a great many temptations in the capital that were not available in the country. She could already see that they kept their wallets in the front pockets of their suit jackets. The pickpockets would love them. Still, she was a Londoner born and bred. She should be able to keep them safe.

"Did you not wish to accompany Peggy this evening?" Lia was dressed for bed in a silken pyjamas and robe. "I am perfectly capable of putting my boys to bed."

"You have had a long, difficult day."

Krista too was dressed for bed. The two women were sitting before the fire in the family room, sipping the hot chocolate Krista had prepared for them.

"I missed having the boys to play with." Krista laughed. "I think I enjoyed bath time tonight as much as they did."

"You were all certainly making enough noise." Lia was thrilled to be back in her own home. She enjoyed time spent with her husband's family but there was no place like home. "Why did you not agree to meet up with Peggy after the boys were safely tucked up in their beds?"

"I am afraid I was having a great deal of difficulty understanding the men's accents. I had to keep asking them to repeat themselves. It was embarrassing." She shrugged. "I thought to save them their blushes. They were so excited about seeing London." She had felt years older than the two young farm hands although both of those men were in their twenties. She had felt ancient before their excited expectation.

"I don't know how they are going to make that long drive tonight in the dark then report for work in the morning." Lia sipped her chocolate, staring into the fire.

"If I understood them correctly," Krista said, "they have agreed that one will sleep in the back of the van while the other drives. They will change over halfway back to Norfolk. They have it all planned and appear delighted with this chance of adventure."

"Yes." Lia sighed mightily. "I heard a great deal of talk about the exciting adventure of war while I was in Norfolk." She remained silent for a moment, her heart heavy at the thought of young men like Bert and Sam marching off to war. It didn't bear thinking about.

"We can't escape the talk of war, can we?" Krista said. "The wireless speaks of nothing else. It appears to me that the world is holding its breath – waiting – or am I being overly dramatic?"

"I don't think so." Lia sighed. "Norfolk is a seaport. The local men are girding themselves for what might come." She sighed deeply. "It was a delightful surprise to the family when we heard Charles would be given a few days off to join us. He arrived by plane. The boys were beside themselves with excitement. They almost drove the poor pilot wild asking questions. We did have some Ministry types visit while my husband was with us. Charles informed me that there were some very heated debates over brandy in the study. Of course, as a female I was not allowed join the company."

Krista remained silent, listening – what could she say?

"I had many meetings with the leaders of the

Women's Institute in Norfolk." Lia sighed. "I am afraid the boys were dreadfully neglected by me over the holiday period." She shrugged. "Still, they had their grandparents and cousins to hand. So, I suppose that is something." She stared across at Krista. "The women of the WI are gearing up for action but, without some guidelines from the powers that be, they can only make the most of what the older members learned from the Great War. The women are as frustrated as we are with the lack of official guidelines, I do assure you."

The two women sat sipping at their cooling drinks, staring into the fire, each lost in her own thoughts.

"We cannot organise the entire country." Lia put her mug on the floor to the side of her chair. She stared across the fire at Krista.

"What are you thinking?" Krista squirmed slightly. The expression on Lia's face was making her uncomfortable.

"Krista, you are young and single. You speak three languages fluently – languages that are going to be in great demand if this wretched war comes to pass." She had heard a great deal of angry muttering about foreigners from countryfolk. It had frightened her – made her fear for her young companion's safety. Who knew what an angry crowd could or would do? "As the mother of a young family, I believe I will not be allowed join any of the active services. I will be expected to sit at home and tend the home fires." She sat forward to glare at Krista. "I refuse to sit and weep. It would drive me insane!"

"You have some idea of what you might do?"

"There is a lady teaching shorthand and typing from her home nearby." Lia knew the woman socially. She had set up the school for gentlewomen to augment her widow's income. The school was very well thought of and supplied secretaries to a great many government departments. "Through our work with the young Jewish orphans we have both seen the great need for women who can type fast and accurately. I believe that need will be vital in the coming days." She waited to see if Krista would comment. When she didn't, Lia continued. She had given a great deal of thought to this matter. "I believe we should both enrol in classes for shorthand and typing. We can attend the classes when the boys are at school." She sat back. "What do you think?"

# Chapter 9

"My dear Lia!" Annora Huxley stared at her guest over the rim of her teacup. She had agreed to meet with Cordelia Caulfield at the other's request. She had not expected this outcome to the meeting.

"Annora, you have been everything that is kind, loaning your students to Rabbi Goldstein. I have watched the young ladies you have loaned to the cause and been astonished at their skill." The well-trained young women sent from this academy had been a godsend in dealing with the mountains of paperwork involved in removing children from danger zones in Europe. "It has made such a difference to have those young women ready and able to take down Krista's translations as she reads them directly from the page.

The speed of each translation has been improved immeasurably." It had also saved poor Krista crippling pain in her hands when she tried to write out each translation in longhand.

"That is all very well, Lia," Annora said, "but it is quite another matter to learn shorthand and typing yourself. It is not usually a skill a lady requires."

"*You* learned well enough to teach others."

"Yes, I did." Annora looked towards the window of the room to the back of her house that she had set aside for her own use. "I learned from a cantankerous old woman who beat our knuckles with a stick if we made an error." She laughed to remember her horror at this abuse. But she and the others had learned – and learned quickly. "When the Great War broke out, the newly established Wrens needed women who could take messages and type swiftly and correctly. I was merely one of the many chosen to take classes." How many times over the years had she thanked her Maker for those lessons? They had saved her sanity and enabled her to support herself and her late husband through difficult times.

"Annora, I want to learn. I do assure you. This is not a whim." Lia had met this woman through the work she'd carried out in helping the removal of young children from countries like Germany and Austria. It was only through conversation she'd discovered that Annora Huxley had been a Wren in the Great War. "I don't know if you are aware that the old guard from the Wrens are gathering in London?"

"I have been contacted by several old friends over the last months. There has been a suggestion that I might close my academy and take up a position within their ranks." Annora stared at her guest, her pale-blue eyes almost shooting sparks. "I am not in a position to volunteer my services. I must earn a living." There was no point in hiding the fact that the school she had set up was keeping the wolf from the door. She lifted the teapot with a suppressed sigh. How she wished she had taken this woman to her kitchen. She could have set the pot on the range to keep it hot. The tea was cooling. She despised cool tea!

"War is coming, Annora." Lia refused more tea with a shake of her head. "We can pray that something will occur to change the course of happenings in Europe. But I would rather be ready to step up and offer my services where needed – hence my desire to learn shorthand and typing. I am also taking driving lessons."

"You have two young children, Lia!" Annora snapped. "They must be your first consideration."

"My boys will always come first in my life. But I cannot and will not sit at home knitting socks while the world around me goes to war. I simply cannot do it!"

"I see." Annora sighed. "You wish to enrol in my day classes?"

"Yes." Lia sat forward. "My boys are in school. They have no need of me during those hours. I wish to enrol both myself and Krista Lestrange in your classes. Krista is fluent in three languages – English, French and German. Her skills will be needed in many quarters. We will apply ourselves to our studies, I do assure you."

"I have met Krista." Annora had been impressed with the skill the young girl displayed in translating letters from heartbroken and desperate parents. "She is foreign, is she not?"

"Krista's parents are deceased," Lia offered. There was no need to go into a great deal of detail. "Her mother was English and a great friend of my sister-in-law Lady Winchester. Her father was French – it was his connections raised and educated Krista."

"Very well." Annora knew she would be a fool to refuse the fees from two extra students for her classes. "There is paperwork to fill out." She stood up, a thin figure dressed all in black, and gestured towards the door. "Let me show you around."

Lea opened the door to her home slowly, a sheaf of papers clutched in one hand. The noise from upstairs drew her out of her introspection. She had been fretting and worrying about her ability to learn new skills. She smiled at the sounds from upstairs. She sometimes thought that Krista and Peggy were as noisy as her two boys as they helped each other around the house.

"*Peggy! Krista!*" she called from the bottom of the stairs. "*Could you come down, please!*" She removed her outer wear of hat, coat and gloves, putting them on the hallstand. She shook out her hair, checking her image in the hallway mirror.

Peggy, almost buried in the sacking cloths she put over her uniform when she cleaned, leaned over the bannister. "Did you need us, Mrs Caulfield?"

"Leave what you're doing, Peggy. I want you and Krista to join me in the kitchen," Lia called over her shoulder as she walked towards the kitchen.

"I heard you calling," Mrs Acers said as soon as her employer appeared in her kitchen. She was up to her oxters peeling vegetables to add to the goose flesh she wanted to put into a casserole. She had the bones of the geese boiling on the range to make stock. She had the fat from the geese she'd roasted boiling down to clarify. She had no time to stop and chat. "Would you not meet with the two girls in the dining room? I'll have young Peggy prepare a pot of tea to take up to you."

"Wilma, there are going to be changes made in the routine of the household." Lia took in the scene in front of her. She knew better than to shock Wilma rigid by offering to help. "You need to know what is happening."

The two young women, Peggy hauling a bucket of dirty water, pushed into the kitchen.

"I will wait until you feel free to sit down over a pot of tea with us." Lia put the papers she held on the table and took a seat out of the way.

"Peggy, as soon as you empty that dirty water out come right back to me," Wilma Acers snapped. "Krista, put the kettle on then gather up these peelings." She pointed a finger towards the peelings on top of her worktable. "Put them in the bucket for the pig man."

Lia watched the three women move around the kitchen, marvelling at their speed and grace. It was almost like a ballet as they restored order to the kitchen. She had not long to wait until they joined her at the table, a pot of tea steaming on a trivet, the table set by Krista with everything they might need.

"I have been to see Mrs Annora Huxley." Lia tapped the papers on the table by her place. "I made enquiries about Krista and me joining her classes. I was fortunate enough to enrol us both in the class that begins this coming Monday. There is a great deal to do before we have all we need." She again tapped the papers. "I have a list of requirements here."

"You are going back to school, Mrs Caulfield?" Peggy was glad of the chance to sit down – she'd been running around all morning restoring order to the top-floor rooms.

"What about the boys?" Krista asked.

"You and I, Krista, will leave the house every morning with the boys. We will drop them at their school before continuing on to our own lessons." Lia made a pretence of consulting the papers. She had studied them already, her stomach in a whirl. Annora had expressed the concern that Lia might be too old to learn all that was needed. She was determined to prove the woman wrong.

"Will you be needing me to pack lunches for you?" Wilma Acers wondered what the world was coming to – were these women not too old to go to school?

"That was what I wished to speak to you about, Wilma. The school is not a great distance from this house. Krista and I will have time to run home for lunch. It would be greatly appreciated if you could have something prepared for us every day on the dot." Lia waited a moment. "What do you think?"

"I'll work up a daily menu." Wilma would enjoy the challenge. She'd have more time on her hands with the mistress out from under her feet but was wise enough not to say that. "What time should I have the lunch ready?"

"We break for an hour at one o'clock," Lia said. "So, one fifteen?"

"I can do that."

"Peggy, will you be able to cope without Krista's help around the house?" Lia asked.

"I will indeed, Mrs Caulfield." Peggy could run through the house with ease when no-one was around to upset her routine. It upset her no end when visitors called to see the mistress when she herself was up to her elbows in cleaning fires and whatnot.

Krista, who had remained silent while the new routine of the house was discussed, now spoke up. "What should we wear?"

"Mrs Huxley was adamant that we should not wear slacks!" Lia smiled. "We will wear skirts and a blouse or twinset to class."

"She's a good soul, that Mrs Huxley," Wilma Acers said suddenly.

"Do you know her, Wilma?" Lia was surprised.

"I know of her more than know her," Wilma said.

"She is well thought of in the back streets," Peggy said.

"Why is that?" Lia waited to hear what the two women had to say. Really, since she had started taking tea in the kitchen with her staff her world had changed.

Wilma received a nod from Peggy to tell the tale, "Well, I don't know if you are aware that poor Mr Huxley was gassed in the Great War."

"So many men were." Lia shook her head, thinking of the poor men walking the streets of London struggling to gasp a breath. It was shameful – shocking.

"Well, Mrs Huxley did something about it." Wilma slapped her hand on the table, rattling the dishes. "She went to the government and forced them to pay for some of those poor creatures to learn how to work in offices instead of tramping the streets begging for crumbs. Found them work with solicitors, doctors and whatnot, I heard tell."

"I haven't heard of this!" Lia exclaimed. "I am afraid I never thought of men taking lessons in shorthand and typing."

"Mrs Huxley offers special rates to pupils from the local schools," Peggy added. "She works with teachers who recommend certain pupils."

"Well, I learn something new every day." Lia shook her head, thinking of the thin, well-corseted figure of Annora Huxley. Who would have guessed the woman was a rebel?

"Yes, indeed." Wilma nodded fiercely. "She's well thought of, is that Mrs Huxley."

"My sister cried every day for a month when she couldn't take up her offer," said Peggy.

"She was offered a place with Mrs Huxley?" Lia enquired.

"She was," Peggy said sadly. "My sister Daisy is a bright spark. She hasn't been the same since she had to go out to work. She was desperate to escape working in the local rag factory but me da wouldn't hear of her continuing on with her schooling." She shrugged. "He said it was a waste of good money to educate girls."

"Unfortunately, that is a commonly held view," Lia said.

"He doesn't know our Daisy," Peggy said. "She's been saving her pennies for years now, hoping to take Mrs Huxley's night classes."

"Has she indeed?" Lia wondered what she could do to help the girl.

"Our Daisy knows what she wants." Peggy too had

been saving pennies to help her sister achieve her dream of escaping the only world they knew. Why should they not have dreams?

# Chapter 10

"In the name of all that's good and holy, Krista Lestrange, what are you wearing?" Wilma Acers stared open-mouthed at the vision standing in her kitchen.

"I told her, Mrs Acers." Peggy stepped into the kitchen behind Krista. "But would she listen to me?"

"I heard you two coming down the stairs." Lia stepped into the kitchen, every inch of her groomed to perfection. She had heard the two young women arguing as they came downstairs. Her curiosity was piqued and she'd decided to see what was happening. She now stood staring at Krista before exchanging a concerned glance with Mrs Acers.

It seemed for a moment no one knew what to say. With a deep breath Lia stepped into the breach.

"Krista, my dear, do you think that is what you should wear to meet Perry's mother for the first time?"

"I have not been invited to take tea with her ladyship." Krista opened her arms and turned slowly to give everyone a full view of her attire. She was clad head to toe in the waterproof garments Perry's mother had chosen for her to wear on her journey through Germany. She had not yet put on the oiled coat and knitted hat but the oiled slacks and heavy jumper with leather elbows and cuffs were strange enough to attract comment.

"You've not been asked to haul a catch of fish neither!" snapped Peggy.

"You have time to change before Perry arrives." Lia glanced at the large kitchen clock to check the time.

"I am not changing my clothes, Lia," Krista insisted. "If I have understood Lady Fotheringham-Carter's invitation correctly – I will be running around muddy fields. I cannot do that wearing cashmere and silk!"

Perry had issued the invitation to meet Lady Fotheringham-Carter – not as his mother but as a woman concerned about the attitude of the young men under her tutelage. Krista was to be used as a guinea pig and she refused to wear clothing that would render any efforts she might make ridiculous.

"But I understood it was your knowledge of languages that had brought you to the attention of Lady Fotheringham-Carter?" Lia asked.

Krista filled a kettle and put it on the range top. She had brought her haversack into the kitchen with her and now removed the flask from it.

"I am unsure of what I can say here." Krista looked at the other women. "Perry is taking me with him to where he has been studying in the country." She thought if it was anything similar to the area where she had been trained before leaving for Germany, the clothes she wore would be ideal. "I want to be prepared for whatever might be asked of me." She walked into the pantry to take out the items she needed to make a snack to take with her.

"This is my kitchen, Krista Lestrange," Wilma stood with her arms crossed over her white apron. "What are you going to do with that lot?" She jerked her head towards the bread and other items Krista carried out of the pantry.

"I plan to take a flask of coffee and some sandwiches with me."

"You have a tongue in your head, don't you?" Wilma snapped. "I could have had everything ready for you if you had only asked."

Lia sat at the large table set to one side of the kitchen. She removed her gold enamelled cigarette case from her skirt pocket. She wasn't willing to leave the kitchen. This was where the action was. She had plans to go shopping this morning. She wanted to purchase the books and other items from the list she'd been given by Annora Huxley. Items she and Krista would need for the classes they were about to take. She needed to get everything done before it was time to pick the boys up from school, but she could delay her departure. She had not yet telephoned for a taxi. She took a cigarette from the case.

Peggy, without being asked, took an ashtray and a box of matches from a shelf by the range. She carried the items to the table, putting them in front of her employer. She waited to see what else needed to be done.

"You are a wonder, Wilma Acers." Krista dared to press a quick kiss onto the other woman's glowering face. "It is not your job to cater to me."

"Get off out of that!" Wilma wiped the kiss off her cheek. "We'll have none of your foreign ways, cheek-kissing and whatnot, in my kitchen. You're in England now." She took the bread out of Krista's hands. "Peggy, get me a tin of salmon out of the pantry. I'll want the ham, as well as two of those lovely apples from the home farm." Wilma cleared a space on her worktable. She began to slice the white loaf thinly. "I'll make the sandwiches. I won't have you shaming my kitchen by taking great big doorstep sandwiches with you, that I won't!" She slapped the breadknife on the tabletop.

Lia hid her smile by putting the cigarette to her lips, hugely entertained once more by the drama taking place in her own home.

"Peggy," Wilma took the goods she'd asked for from Peggy's hands, "you can bring out that Dundee Cake I made and all. You can put a few slices of that in your haversack, Krista. Perry is very fond of my Dundee Cake."

"I would enjoy a pot of tea and a slice of your delicious Dundee Cake myself." Lia puffed happily. Mrs Acers guarded the fruit cake topped by silvered almonds. She brought it out for company but never for the twins. They were not yet old enough to enjoy the cake's wonderful richness of flavour.

"Peggy ..."

"I'll see to it, Mrs Acers," Peggy said before the

instruction to make a pot of tea and set the table could be stated aloud. "It's all go in this house this morning."

"I couldn't believe my eyes when you drove up in this old girl." Krista gave the steering wheel of the campervan a fond pat. She was driving through the streets of London, heading inland at Perry's direction.

"Mother has been in discussion with Captain Waters." Perry sat in the passenger seat, a smile on his face. "It was felt your arrival at the wheel of this large vehicle would set the tone they wanted for your introduction to the camp."

"What exactly is expected of me today, Perry?" Krista kept her eyes on the road. She was happy to be back at the wheel. Apart from anything else it gave her something to do and saved her from fretting all through the journey. She was nervous about what would be asked of her. Perry had not seemed dismayed by the outfit she was wearing. He'd smiled but insisted she bring a complete change of clothing with her. He'd sat in the kitchen while Krista packed an overnight bag.

"I don't know, Krista – truly." Perry shifted. "Take a left at the next intersection."

There was silence while she followed his instructions. They had left the busy streets of London behind and were driving through narrow country lanes. She had no idea where she was but the countryside around her was green and beautiful even in its winter slumber.

"How are your lessons going?" Krista snapped in German.

"It is difficult," Perry answered in the same language. He lit a cigarette, opening the window at his side to allow the smoke to escape. "I have something of an advantage after travelling with you through Germany." He was slow but precise she was pleased to hear. "I hated being out of the loop when we travelled. It is vital to understand what is being said around you. A lot of the men I am training with fail to understand that."

"Surely knowledge of a foreign language was considered vital when choosing the men being trained?" Krista said in French. She already knew the answer. Peggy had been astonished to discover that the men Perry was training with were all from the upper classes. She'd had quite a bit to say on the subject.

Krista slowed the campervan down when she noticed two white shapes moving along the verge, nibbling on the grass growing there. Some farmer had a fence down.

"We are coming up to a main road," Perry said in French. "You will be turning to the left when we reach it. As to your question, you already know that there is a problem teaching the men to actually speak the languages. We, all of us, have had quite extensive classroom lessons in each language but there are very few of us who can speak with ease."

Krista would have been content to continue grilling Perry in his language progress but he turned to her and switched back to English.

"How do you do it, Krista?" he asked. "I watched you change languages with ease. It never seemed to bother you." He puffed smoke out the window. "We need to know how to do that."

"Perry," Krista sighed, "it is not easy. When we were in Germany there were times I wanted to scream at you to speak French just to give my poor battered brain a rest."

"Truly?"

"Yes, of course!" Krista snapped in English. "We were both under a great deal of strain. It was obvious from the moment we arrived in Germany that we were in enemy territory. I had to switch between German and English at a moment's notice – neither of which is my mother tongue. I sometimes felt as if my brain would pour out of my ears at the end of a difficult day."

"You have no idea how happy I am to hear that."

"I am so glad I can make you happy." Krista grinned and nudged him with her elbow. "Where are we going now? Are we almost there?" She had been driving for some time and to her eyes they were surrounded by wilderness.

"You need to slow down." Perry straightened in his seat. "We will be turning off this road onto a country lane. The entrance is difficult to see if you don't know it is there."

A few moments later he directed her to turn off the road onto a muddy lane. The campervan bounced into and out of holes in the track. Krista kept her eyes peeled but still could not see any sign of inhabitants. They were in the middle of nowhere with miles of long grass and a great many trees blocking her vision. Where on earth was this camp?

"Slow down and prepare to stop!" Perry snapped suddenly.

Krista stared as a guard post appeared as they crested a hill. Two soldiers stood at a metal bar stretched across the track.

"That is ridiculous," she muttered under her breath as the campervan slowed and rolled towards the barrier. "It would be a simple matter to drive around that thing."

"Only if you want the guards to shoot you," Perry replied softly.

"They might shoot the van with their handguns but they wouldn't hit me if I stepped on the accelerator."

"They might not but the snipers hidden in the woods would." Perry waved at the two soldiers, men he knew by sight. He reached into his inside pocket for the papers needed to grant them access to the camp.

Krista rolled down her window and waited.

"Would you step out of the van, please, miss?" One of the soldiers approached the driver's side of the vehicle. The other stayed by the barrier, his hand on his sidearm.

"They are more polite than the Germans anyway," Krista said to Perry as she opened the door, preparing to step down out of the van.

"You might want to put your hat on." Perry put a hand on her arm, stopping her from exiting the vehicle. He passed a woollen knit cap to Krista. "I have our papers here, sergeant!" he said to the soldier holding the driver's door open. He held the orders out of the open passenger window, waiting for the soldier to walk around the vehicle and examine them.

Krista was staring at the hat. "Don't be ridiculous."

"*Please*," Perry insisted.

With a shrug she complied and, while the sergeant turned to walk around the front of the campervan, she pulled the hat down over her head.

"*Achtung!*" Perry bit out in German. It was the only warning he was allowed to give her.

# Chapter 11

Krista stepped out of the campervan as if she had not heard Perry's warning. She closed the door of the van at her back and took a wide step away. She did not want to become trapped against the van. She stretched her arms up to the sky, her eyes searching for danger, her ears listening for anyone creeping up on her. Growing up, the eldest Dumas brothers delighted in trapping Krista and hurting her out of sight of their parents. The training she'd received from Captain Waters and his men had honed her skill to avoid injury.

There was a rustling in the long grass to the side of the dirt track where the campervan was parked. Out of the corner of her eye she was aware of Perry and the two guards watching her. With a hoarse scream a man exploded from the grass, running towards Krista with a grimace on his dirt-streaked face, his helmet sprouting greenery, his uniform designed to blend in with the scenery.

She did not see a gun in his outstretched hands. She waited until he was almost upon her before taking a step aside and forward onto her left leg. She lifted her booted right foot and brought it down sharply on the the knee of his standing leg. He went flying backwards onto the ground.

The man was soon back on his feet. *"That's a woman!"* With his hands in the air, he backed away from Krista.

"And you are dead, Dawson."

Captain Waters walked out of the trees, much to Krista's relief. He was followed by a group of men and a small woman dressed in a fashion very similar to Krista's.

"I informed you, did I not, Dawson, when you volunteered to plan this offensive," the woman bit out, "that the driver of the campervan should be approached with caution."

"You didn't tell me it was a woman," Dawson muttered, spitting grit from his teeth onto the grass.

The woman gave the soldier a disgusted look. The tone of her voice withering. "That is immaterial. If the driver of the van had been armed, you would have been dead before you completed your first comic-book hero yell."

"Gentlemen," Captain Waters shook his head in disgust, "we gave you the freedom to plan this mission. Allow me to tell you it has been a complete disaster."

How could they train these men to understand that every moment they were on a mission would be a matter of life and death? They seemed to be all about drinking and having a good time. He wished to heaven he could get rid of the lot of them and start again.

Krista was ordered to park the campervan on a field dotted with Nissan huts that stretched as far as the eye could see. There was a large house built on a hillock in the distance. Soldiers marched around the fields.

There was a sharp rap on the campervan door before it was opened.

"Krista, we have not been introduced. I am Lady Fotheringham-Carter." The woman Krista had seen earlier stood in the open doorway. "I believe you know my son Peregrine. May I come in?"

"Certainly, your ladyship."

"Please call me Beryl." The shorter woman stepped up into the body of the campervan.

"Would you care for a cup of coffee?" Krista wanted something to do with her hands. She couldn't stand here like a lump on a log. She wished Perry were here but he'd been ordered back to his group. "I have only black, I'm afraid." She'd checked the cupboards. The cold box was empty.

"That would be delightful." Beryl took a seat on the bench under the window and watched the young woman who so fascinated her son arrange a table, set out mugs and side plates with minimum fuss. She longed to scream with frustration. Why couldn't she have a group of women like this one to train instead of the bumbling Hurrah Henrys that had been foisted upon her?

"I packed a snack before leaving home." Krista opened her haversack, removing the items she'd stored there, including her flask. She poured piping hot coffee into the mugs and passed one to her guest.

"Krista," Beryl inhaled the delightful aroma of coffee while staring over the mug at the younger woman, "Peregrine is much taken with you, my dear."

Krista said nothing. She was hungry. She arranged the sandwiches so lovingly prepared by Mrs Acers onto a large plate and put them on the table. She reversed the driver's seat until it faced the body of the campervan and took a seat.

"You are exactly what is needed here." Beryl didn't pursue the subject of her son's interest in this young woman. Now was not the time nor the place. She selected a salmon sandwich and put it on her side plate. "You speak three European languages fluently to hear Peregrine and Captain Waters tell it. You are aware of your surroundings – quick to act. There is but one problem ..."

"I am female."

"I had hoped that attitude had died a natural death during the Great War." Beryl bit into the sandwich almost savagely. "I and others like me had to fight every single day to prove we had the skills needed to do our jobs. There were days when I thought I would go insane constantly fighting for my place in the war effort – now this!" She flung her hand towards the exterior of the campervan. "I am right back where I started – silently screaming and cursing at what feels like the same stubborn, mule-headed – *males*!"

Krista drank her coffee and ate the sandwiches.

What could she say? The attitude of the men in this camp should not have come as a surprise to a married woman who had an adult son and several stepsons.

Beryl took another sandwich. "I am trying not to scream and swear but, dear Lord, it is tempting."

A knock on the campervan door surprised them. The door opened and Captain Waters appeared in the opening.

"May I come inside or have you both had enough of the male of the species?"

"Do join us, Graham," Beryl said. "Before I singe poor Krista's ears off."

"Good to see you again, Krista." Graham Waters stepped up into the campervan.

"Coffee, captain?" Krista held up the flask.

"Thank you." Graham Waters took a mug from the cupboard before joining Lady Fotheringham-Carter on the bench seat. Making himself at home – he did own the campervan after all. He put the mug on the table, waiting for Krista to fill it.

"That little exercise was a fiasco," Graham bit out. "And so I have told the men."

"Pinned their ears back, did you?" Beryl smiled.

"If it were not so tragic I would laugh." Graham gulped his coffee.

"What did you hope to achieve with this morning's happenings?" Krista asked the two people sitting on the bench.

"You may as well tell her, Graham," Beryl said. "Krista has already proved that she will not speak of confidential matters. She may well have some insights we could use."

After a moment of silence, the captain nodded and with a sigh began. "Perry and the young men you saw this morning are being trained to lead groups of men into Europe – we wish them to gather information. We cannot use trained soldiers. We have tried with fatal results. The soldiers simply cannot shake off their training and appear as harmless civilians." Graham shook his head. "This group is a disaster as you have seen. We cannot convince them that they must be alert at every moment. They appear to believe this is all a great adventure. Perry wrote so glowingly of you in his report on your mission to retrieve my sister that I thought …"

The women remained silent as he paused.

"I had hoped seeing you – a female – take one of their own down, would serve as a kick in the backside to those men."

"Without consulting me!" Krista almost slammed her mug onto the tabletop. "You expected me to perform like a trained monkey." She glared at the captain. "Would that be correct?"

"As he said, we hoped using you in such a way would shake some sense into our young men." Beryl buried her smile in the coffee mug. She knew she was throwing gasoline on a fire. Perry's young woman was furious, and rightly so.

"Captain Waters, you have used and abused me for the last time." Krista had enough of men using her. The Grey Man wanted her to spy for him. Waters wanted to turn her into a performing monkey. No, she had had quite enough.

"I say!" Waters objected.

"I have a great deal to say but you have never had

the courtesy to ask me. If at any time you would care to ask for and listen to my opinion – do contact me for an appointment." She stormed out of the campervan before she could say anything more. She needed to collect herself.

Krista smiled and accepted the glass of champagne Perry took from a passing waiter. The cream lace dress she wore swept the top of her shoes as he led her around the large music room. A young cadet sat playing music softly at a grand piano. She had been given a room in the country mansion that was being used as command centre. A smiling country maid had been ordered to assist her. Once more she'd been groomed within an inch of her life. She would have preferred to return to London. Earlier Lady Fotheringham-Carter had followed her from the campervan and insisted she dine with them. She was conscious of a great many male eyes following her every movement. There were very few women present.

"You look delightful," Perry said, leading her in the direction of a group of young men in evening dress. They stood out in the company of men in uniform, awards and merits gleaming on their chests. He leaned in to whisper, "What have you done to Captain Waters? The man is positively glaring at you."

"I ..."

Before she could say more a short gnome of a man appeared at their side, white hair standing out around his face like a halo, gesticulating wildly, German words exploding out of his mouth. He was accompanied by an elegantly groomed man who was his direct opposite in appearance. It would have been amusing if he too were not gesticulating and demanding attention in French!

"Krista," Perry said, "sort this out, would you?"

"If I might assist," Krista said in German and then in French, uncomfortably aware of the discreet attention being paid to this section of the room.

While the short German pointed at the Frenchman, words spewing from his lips at machine-gun speed, Krista translated his rant into French almost simultaneously hoping her calm tones would reduce the tension between the two men.

The Frenchman shouted his replies and rebuttals in between the German's words. Krista stepped slightly away from both men, searching in vain for somewhere to put down her champagne glass. She continued to change languages at speed, translating the argument taking place between the two men as they argued the merits of their respective armament designs. Perry took the glass from her hand.

The argument between the two men had degenerated. They were now shouting insults.

Krista held up both hands and stopped translating. "We are going off topic," she said in French and German, refusing to stand here translating each man's opinion of the other's intelligence.

The sound of a single slow handclap attracted everyone's attention.

Captain Waters, smiling widely, walked over to join Krista. "That, gentlemen – is what we require of you."

"*Fraulein*," the German man clicked his heels and bent over Krista's hand, "thank you for your assistance."

He spoke in what to Krista's ears was unaccented English, his blue eyes twinkling in his wrinkled face.

"*Mademoiselle*, you do our country proud," the Frenchman said with a laugh, his English flowing freely.

"I say," one of the twelve young men protested, "that is very unfair. This woman has obviously received intensive coaching in translation."

Krista fumed as she realised that Captain Waters had once more made use of her.

A gong sounded loudly to signal to the company to finish their drinks and make their way to the dining room.

"Just a second." Dawson, the man she had knocked on his face, raised his voice to be heard. "You cannot leave it like that. I want to know where you found this young woman. She is obviously a skilled interpreter. What arm of the government does she work for? If they have men employed with such skills, surely they should be here with us?"

"Krista, would you care to answer Dawson?" Waters put his glass on the tray a waiter held aloft waiting for the used glasses.

"Mr Dawson," Krista addressed the indignant man as she accepted the gracefully offered bent elbow of her countryman, then spoke over her shoulder as she was led away, "I am currently employed as a nanny to twin boys of five in London."

# Chapter 12

"Where on earth can we put them?" Lia, Peggy by her side, was walking through the downstairs rooms of her London home. "I placed an order for two typewriting machines to be delivered to the house. Krista and I need to practise our typewriting skills. It is unfortunate that our free time seems to so often coincide, therefore we are agreed that one machine to share between us would simply not suffice." She stood in the family room, wondering where they could put the machines that would keep them safe from her twin son's inquisitive fingers. She knew the boys would find the machines fascinating – but they were not toys!

"If I might make a suggestion." Peggy wanted to move things along. Krista had taken Edward and

David to the park. They would be full of energy when they returned, running around the place. She couldn't keep walking from room to room while her mistress hemmed and hawed.

"I would be glad of any suggestion." Lia sighed.

"There is that room off the kitchen where we keep the big chairs and whatnot that we can pull out into the kitchen ..." Peggy began.

"We couldn't sit typing in that dark room!" Lia protested.

"No, no, that is not what I am thinking. Let me show you." Sometimes you had to practically take the mistress by the hand and show her what you were talking about. She led the way into the kitchen, Lia following on her heels.

Mrs Acers didn't stop in her work when the mistress of the house stepped into her domain. It was becoming a common occurrence. One she couldn't like. It was not right, the mistress visiting the kitchen, but what could she do or say about it? It wasn't her place to question the mistress.

"We'll not get under your feet, Mrs Acers." Peggy knew Mrs Acers disliked having her Saturday routine disturbed. She didn't come in on Sunday but left everything prepared for Peggy to cook for the family Sunday lunch. She always said she did two days' work in one day. "I just want to show the mistress something." She didn't wait for a response but walked to a room on one side of the chimney breast that wrapped around the big black range. The room was deep and dark. She reached in and pulled the cord to turn on the one lightbulb hanging from the ceiling. It did nothing to brighten the space.

"As I said," Lia leaned over Peggy's shoulder, looking into the dark room, "we couldn't possibly work in here. Apart from anything else, we would freeze."

"No, no!" Peggy protested again. She stepped into the room and waved her arms around. "If we had Mr Woods the carpenter make up a table on casters that you could wheel in and out, you could put the two machines on top of the table and wheel it into the kitchen to practise. When the boys are in bed, Mrs Acers has returned to her own home. The kitchen will be empty and toasty warm from the range. You and Krista could work away to your hearts' content. We'd only have to push the machines back in here and the kitchen would be ready for the next day's work."

"Peggy," Lia smiled, "that is a wonderful idea! It will solve quite a number of problems. I will send for Mr Woods at once. What a very clever young woman you are!" She clapped her hands in delight. She hurried out of the kitchen to find the telephone number for Woods the carpenter's workshop. She wanted that table as soon as possible.

Mrs Acers was peeling potatoes, carrots, and swedes into bowls of cold water. The vegetables would be stored overnight in the pantry, ready to be cooked the following day. She had a lovely cut of beef to go with them. Peggy would have to make the Yorkshire pudding and gravy fresh tomorrow. Mrs Acers had taught her how. She'd have preferred to cook the meal herself but she did love her Sundays off. She laughed under her breath. What woman ever truly had a day off? She had her family's meals to cook and her own house to put in order.

"Well, Miss Clever Clogs, now that you've solved the problems of the world would you take the milk and chocolate out of the pantry, please? Krista and the boys can have a hot drink and a slice of one of the apple pies I baked, to keep them going." She pressed her hands into her back and looked around her kitchen. "I suppose they will have it in the kitchen and all. I don't know what the world is coming to when the gentry keep stepping into my kitchen." She shook her head, returning to her work.

"It amazes me that those two lads will want to eat again!" Peggy called from the pantry. "They had a big lunch not that long ago."

"Young lads are bottomless pits when it comes to eating and drinking." Wilma began to restore order to her worktable. "You can carry them bowls into the pantry when you have a minute, Peggy. I'm putting the kettle on for a pot of tea – me mouth is that dry I'm spitting feathers."

"Just a minute, David, Edward." Krista was standing outside the front door of the house, her two charges red-faced and panting after their race to be first home. "We need to remove these muddy wellington boots before we step into the hall."

She knelt down to assist in the removal of the black rubber boots each boy wore. The boots were liberally decorated with muck and dead leaves. Peggy would have a fit if the boys dirtied her clean floors.

"I know Peggy waxed the entrance hall this morning," she whispered conspiratorially to the grinning boys.

106

She opened the door, holding it for a moment while she checked that each foot was dry and warm in the thick knitted woollen socks the boys wore under their boots. "You can do the 'Skaters' Waltz' while I remove my boots – but wait for me before going upstairs." She watched them while she removed her own wellington boots. She left the three pairs of boots standing to one side of the wide doorway to dry. She would scrape them clean when she had the twins organised.

"Remember, you must have music for the waltz." She joined the twins in their gleeful dance across the waxed hallway, humming along: "*Da da da dum! Da da da dum!*" With a boy by each hand she showed them how to skate to the music.

"Well," Lia stood in the open doorway of the drawing room, smiling to see her son's enjoyment, "this looks delightful."

"*Mama, we are skating!*" Edward shouted.

"*Krista has taught us how!*" David said.

"When we are good skaters, Krista is going to take us to the ice-skating rink in Hammersmith!"

"We have to practise hard and be good boys!" David followed Krista's hand movements and allowed himself to be twirled around, his little face almost split by his wide grin.

"Why don't I give Krista a hand removing your coats?" Lia stepped into the gleaming white-and-black-tiled hallway. "The hall is warm and you will have more freedom of movement without your heavy coats."

"Take off your shoes, Mama, and skate with us." Edward pulled at his mother's hand. "Come on – you can skate with us! Krista will show you how. But you must move to the music. Krista will hum for you."

Lia and Krista helped the boys out of their hats, coats, gloves, scarfs and left the items on the stairs to be carried up when they had finished having fun. She kicked off her shoes, preparing to join in. Krista began to hum and with a boy each they travelled around the hallway to the shouts of the boys that quite overshadowed the music of the 'Skaters' Waltz' that Lia and Krista were humming.

Peggy came out of the kitchen to see what was going on. She laughed to see her employer behaving as she and her brothers and sisters had when they were young enough to believe they were helping their mother by polishing the hall lino.

She returned to the kitchen without disturbing the skaters to inform Mrs Acers that they were not yet ready for the hot chocolate to be prepared.

"I've left you your instructions, Peggy." Wilma Acers was removing her white apron. She would carry her aprons home and bleach them this evening. "I ordered cream from the milkman. It's in the pantry. There is no need for you to make custard to go with the apple pie I've left for dessert. You will be busy enough making the Yorkshire pud and gravy. It is a lot to ask of a young girl but needs must." Wilma gave a sigh as she pushed her arms into her coat.

Peggy stood listening politely. She had heard it all before but Wilma would fret over her kitchen when she was not here to rule it.

"I've left instructions for the roast." Wilma pulled her hat over her greying head of curls. She'd have to get her young neighbour to come in and give her a permanent one of these evenings. "Put the roast into the range oven before you go to early Mass. You will need to add the potatoes and veg as soon as you come back. Mind now …" She looked around to see if she'd forgotten anything. She continued to bark out instructions as she prepared herself to step out into the cold day. She would have to rush to get all of her shopping done. With a martyred sigh, she patted Peggy on the shoulder and took her leave.

"I'm away now, Mrs Caulfield." Wilma kept herself well out of the way of the shouting, laughing people in the hallway. She raised her eyes up to heaven at the shenanigans. "Peggy has her orders." She pulled open the door, her mind buzzing with all she needed to get done before she could put her feet up and relax.

"Thank you, Mrs Acers." Lia didn't stop skating Edward around. "We will see you Monday. Give my best to your family."

"I'll do that." Wilma pulled the door closed behind her, sniffed in disgust at the dirty boots by the side of the door and, with her head held high, her shopping bag over her arm, she turned her mind to her own wants and needs.

"Peggy, join us, do." Lia sat at the kitchen table, waiting for Krista and the boys to return from upstairs. It was nice not to have Wilma staring daggers at her for forgetting her place.

Peggy was watching the pot of milk she had on top of the range. She did not want it to boil over. There was nothing worse – in her opinion – then the smell of burnt milk and the mess it made to clean up. She had the block of chocolate grated, ready to add to the milk. The table was set for four with heavy-weight porcelain mugs and plates. The lads were murder on delicate china.

"I will slice this delicious-looking apple pie while you set a place for yourself at the table, Peggy." Lia stood to slice the pie.

Peggy put the pot to one side of the range with a suppressed sigh. She'd more to do than sitting chatting at the table but it wasn't her place to go against the mistress's wishes. She was hoping to get away this evening to visit her family.

Krista and the twins walked into the kitchen. The faces and hands of the twins gleamed moistly from the scrubbing Krista had given them. Their hair was for once sitting down on their heads. It wouldn't last but at this moment they looked like little angels.

# Chapter 13

Later that same evening while the boys were asleep in bed – Peggy had left to visit her family – Krista and Lia sat before the fire in the dimly lit drawing room, their stocking feet resting on the rim of the brass fender.

"I cannot believe it is almost Sunday again." Lia rested her head against the chair back. "This week passed so quickly. I hope you have made plans for your day off. The boys and I have been invited out for afternoon tea with a friend and her children." She was rambling, not really thinking about what she was saying. "The boys will enjoy spending time with their friends, I'm sure. I don't know what time we will return." She was silent for a moment. "I hope you too enjoy yourself tomorrow, Krista."

"Thank you," Krista muttered. What else could she say? It was nice to get a break from two energetic little boys but everything was closed on Sunday. She would take herself out though. She'd discovered that if she remained in the house there was always some little thing she might take care of or a chore she could lend a hand with.

"Krista," Lia stared across the fire at the younger woman, "I am afraid I am too old to learn all that is being taught to us. I have never felt so dim-witted in my life as I have this past week."

"Lia, you are demanding too much of yourself," Krista objected.

"The frustration of trying to understand all of those squiggles in the shorthand course workbook has brought me to screaming point." This was the first time they had truly been able to sit and discuss their first week of school. Lia had spent several evenings meeting up with friends she'd missed over the holiday season. When she was free Krista had spent her evenings assisting the local Rabbi in his endeavours to remove Jewish children and their families from the threatening war in Europe.

"I have spoken at length with Vera Conklin ..." Krista hid her yawn behind a hand.

"Do I know the woman?"

"Vera is one of the women assisting in the work of translating and typing up the letters Rabbi Goldstein is receiving, in greater numbers every day it seems. She is a marvel to observe. Her shorthand speed is breath-taking. The volume of letters I can translate has improved immensely with her aid. She makes no errors in transcribing her notes with the typewriter. I have been astonished by her skill."

"I have begun to doubt my ability to learn what our teachers are trying so hard to teach us." Lia couldn't meet Krista's eyes. She was floundering in class.

"Vera laughed almost hysterically when I mentioned my own difficulties in learning shorthand and typing to her. She appeared to think that someone who can translate between three different languages fluently should have no difficulty understanding all of those darn squiggles." Krista smiled across at Lia. She had thought she was the only one experiencing terror at her inability to understand the lessons being taught.

"Truly, Krista?" Lia gasped. "I am not alone in my struggle to learn?"

"Lia," Krista again tried to hide a yawn, "we have run back to this house at lunch hour every day this past week." She paused for a moment, wondering if she had the right to make suggestions of change to her employer. "Vera suggests that we take a packed lunch and share the free time with our fellow students. She guarantees that each one is experiencing the same confusion as ourselves. She said she herself experienced the reassurance that can be found in sharing your troubles with your fellow students."

"But you have said that this Vera is a marvel to observe?" Lia was afraid to hope. She had felt so inferior to the other students this week – all of whom were younger than she.

"Yes, indeed, Vera said she was at her wits' end in the early days of her studies." Krista pulled her feet up onto the seat. She was afraid she was going to fall asleep here. The heat from the fire and the comfort of the soft chair were not helping her fight her tiredness. It had been a difficult week and a long day running after two active boys. She wanted her bed. "According to Vera we will reach a point – each in our own time – where the squiggles begin to make sense to us."

"I sincerely hope this is true. I have been feeling quite demoralised."

"We can only do our best." Krista yawned again. "I am sorry, Lia, I must away to my bed. I am falling asleep where I sit."

"Yes, indeed." Lia felt more hopeful. "It is late. Peggy is not yet back. I don't like to think of her walking the streets in the dark."

"One of her brothers escorts her back to this house from the family home." Krista didn't know if she should wait to tend the fire or go to bed, leaving Lia to take care of the chore before she went up to her own bed.

"Yes," Lia said slowly, "I suppose I knew that." She stared into the glowing coals. "Goodnight, Krista, sleep well." She wanted to sit here and think.

"Goodnight." Krista pushed her feet into her slippers before leaving the room.

"Good morning, Peggy." Krista was in the kitchen pouring coffee into a flask when Peggy, yawning widely, joined her.

"What in the name of goodness are you doing up at this hour of the morning?" Peggy put the kettle on – she needed a pot of tea before she felt human. "This is your one day to have a lie-in."

"I didn't sleep very well, Peggy." Krista put the cap

on the flask. "I am in a mood so I am going to take my cranky self out for a long walk."

"What about your breakfast? You'll be weak with hunger if you leave the house without bit, bite, nor sup. Nowhere is open today as you well know. It's Sunday, for heaven's sake."

"I have had a mug of coffee." Krista put the flask into her haversack. "That will do me fine for the moment." She began to leave the kitchen. "If I am not back for lunch just put a covered plate in the warmer for me and go home to your family. I will see you later." She didn't wait for Peggy to argue. She had to get out of the house.

She took her coat, hat, scarf and gloves from where she had draped them over the hallstand on her way to the kitchen. She quickly pulled the outdoor garments over her slacks and sweater. She folded the leg of her slacks over before pulling her wellington boots on. She didn't care what she looked like. She wanted to be as warm as possible. In no time at all she was dressed for the weather and out the door.

She walked along the damp gas-lamp-lit streets. There were very few people out and about. She was making for the path that bordered the park. She lowered her chin into her scarf and, with her haversack on her back, her gloved hands buried in the deep pockets of her coat, she quick-marched along the pavement. She didn't care that it was cold and miserable. She had a destination in mind. She had told no one of the oasis of peace she had discovered on one of her many solitary Sunday walks. She walked swiftly along when she reached the path, smiling as her wellington boots kicked at the puddles sitting on the tar-covered path. It had been raining for days. The trees were dropping with the weight of water on their bare branches. The grass area was water-logged.

The rain became heavier, the wind lashing the water into her face as she struggled to keep her speed up – she did not want to be late. She lifted her head to check her location, almost blinded by the water that blew into her face. She was almost there. She blinked the water off her lashes as she continued to struggle on, determined to be on time.

She checked traffic before stepping off the path into the road. She crossed the wide street towards the large estates that marched along on the opposite side of the parkway. Each estate was guarded by high red-brick walls, gleaming black iron gates firmly locked against the hoi polloi, breaking up the length of red brick. She almost ran around the block, splashing unheeding into puddles. She reached a laneway that bordered the rear entrances of the estates. Here too red-brick walls guarded the privacy of the people sitting in high style behind them. The walls were lower and the gates were wooden. She stopped at a familiar spot when she was almost halfway down the laneway. She ignored the water pouring down from the overhanging tree and settled with her back to the wall – waiting.

Soon the sound of glorious voices chanting travelled to where she stood. With her head bowed she listened to music that spoke to her soul. Her tears fell as she heard the men chanting aloud, accompanied by organ music. They were chanting in liquid French. She stood lost to her surroundings, enjoying the magic of the moment. She stood as she had so many times before, unaware of the passing of time until the music reached a soaring crescendo. She took a deep breath, preparing to step away from the wall.

"What do you here?" A young man dressed in postulant's grey robes stood before her, holding a large black umbrella over his head, his bare feet in leather sandals. "This is not first time."

"You may speak French if it suits you." Krista blinked the water from her lashes.

"You are female!" he exclaimed in French. "Yet you dress as a boy. I ask again, what do you do here?"

"I listen." Krista pushed her body upright.

"Come, the Abbot wishes to speak with you." The man grabbed hold of her elbow before she could leave.

"Why?"

"I do not question the abbot. I obey." The young man pulled her gently but firmly towards the door cut into the high wooden gate.

Krista shrugged and followed along. She stepped through the door and into a garden sleeping under a coat of wet straw. She recognised support canes standing bare in the garden and wondered briefly what grew in the large expanse. She had expected lawn. She was escorted in the direction of a building that must have once served as a stable block to judge from its outward appearance. When the monk pushed open the door, she was surprised to see a paved surface. Monks in long white robes, their hoods pulled over their heads, arms folded over their stomachs, hands buried under their vestments, moved over the surface without paying any attention to Krista and her escort.

"What is this place?" Krista whispered. The building

seemed to defy anyone to make noise.

"We are a small community of French Benedictine monks," was the answer she received as she was towed towards a staircase.

They stopped in front of the first door set into a long corridor of closed doors.

"This is the abbot's cell."

Her escort knocked and was told to enter. He opened the door and they stood in the doorway.

"The person you requested is here, monseigneur," the young monk said in French, making no attempt to enter.

"English, Gaston!" A heavy-set man, iron-grey hair shaved close to his head, bright-brown eyes staring, a look of amusement on his handsome face, was sitting behind a desk almost buried in papers. "English!" He waved a hand. "You may enter."

"We are wet and muddy, monseigneur," Gaston objected.

"That is of no matter. Enter." The abbot waved them forward.

Krista was pulled into the room, her wet boots squelching on the gleaming wooden floors.

"The female is French, monseigneur." Gaston stood almost to attention before the desk of his leader.

"Female … indeed." The abbot stared in surprise for a moment only. "And French. Then by all means let us speak French."

To Be Continued